C000071051

Adequate Counsel

A Novel by O. R. Johnson

This book is a work of fiction. Names, characters, places, and incidents are the product of the author's imagination or are used fictitiously. Any resemblance to actual events, locales, or persons, living or dead, is coincidental.

Copyright © 2016 by O.R. Johnson

All rights reserved. Except as permitted under the U.S. Copyright Act of 1976 no part of this publication may be reproduced, distributed, or transmitted in any form or by any means, or stored in a database or retrieval system, without the prior written permission of the publisher.

ISBN: 978-0-692-64867-4

Dedication

To my mother, Reba McCollum for inspiring the character Nadine and giving me my wings to fly.

Acknowledgements

Thank you to every family member, friend, devoted reader, and internet stranger that read the sneak peaks of this book and pushed me to complete it. This story was challenging to write, your support pushed me to keep going.

A very special thanks goes to Charita C, Kristie R, Kristin B, EJ Cole, Kenya B, Ingrid C, Nadeen C- Each of you encouraged me at a time when I desperately needed it! I acknowledge and thank my awesome children- you guys are a type of motivation only a parent can understand. I pray that you are as proud to call me your mother as I am to call you my children. My most humble appreciation goes to the man that keeps me lifted and pushes me to never stop pursuing my dreams, my husband Lyndell.

October 2015

9:00 am

Michael sat rubbing his temples with his fingers.
Everything about the tiny room made his entire body
ache. The smell of lemon furniture polish that
covered all of the furniture caused his stomach to
churn. He stood to put some distance between the
wooden table and his nostrils. As he walked over to
the window for the third time in the last half hour, he
was once again reminded of the gravity of the verdict
he was waiting to hear. Although the news crews
couldn't see him, he could see the trucks from every
local news station and a few national ones parked on
the street. Charlotte, North Carolina hadn't received
this much attention since the Rae Carruth case.
Something about high profile murder cases seemed to
draw the journalistic vultures to the city.

Everyone knew the jury was back. Everyone was waiting to hear the verdict that would change his client's life forever. Just a year ago he'd been in a similar situation, but strangely he felt nowhere near as confident as he did then. His previous client was a strong professional football player, not a fragile young girl with her whole life ahead of her. He rubbed his fingers through his thick dark hair, a nervous tick he'd picked up while working on this case. Michael turned to look at his client Shamika who, despite the seriousness of the charge she was facing, looked quite calm. Her dark skin was smooth and clear. Her hair was styled the same way each time he saw her, pulled into a tight ponytail. Her frame was thin, a fact which Michael attributed to the stress of the case. He worried about her. She should be out giggling about boys, not facing first degree murder charges. Michael shook his head swiftly and began to speak to his client.

"How are you feeling Shamika?"

She looked down at her feet before responding. "I'm nervous. I don't want to go to prison for the rest of my life. Who is going to take care of my baby if they lock me up?"

"Don't worry about that right now. You have to think positively."

Shamika's searching eyes shot up to meet Michael's stare. "I want to, but I read on the internet that long deliberations mean they'll find me guilty. It took them ten days," she said in a tiny voice that clearly revealed her youth.

Michael smiled. Even though Shamika was worried, knowing his teenage client took the time to research court proceedings proved to him that the last year of his life had meaning. The girl he met a year ago could barely read and was too afraid to speak to anyone. Despite the outcome of the case he knew her life was enriched because of his efforts. He imagined this to be how a father feels when he learns his child has accomplished a great feat. The almond shaped eyes that stared back at him were not those of his flesh and blood, but he hoped to one day see the same trust in the eyes of his future children.

"I'm happy to hear that you did your research Shamika, but I assure you, the internet does not know whether or not that jury believes us or the prosecutor."

"What if the jury believes the prosecutor?"

Michael walked to his client and squatted down in front of her. Using his right index finger he lifted her head so that she could look him in the eyes.

"Shamika, I know you are scared, but the evidence in this case was clear. We presented a strong case. Let's try to trust the justice system to get this one right."

A single tear rolled from Shamika's left eye and down her cheek as she nodded her head.

"Trust me. No matter how this turns out, I will not stop until you are free to finish growing up and raising your baby. Besides, you promised me you were going to finish high school and go to college," Michael said with a smile.

Though more tears now streamed down her face, Shamika returned the smile.

Their moment was interrupted by a knock on the door.

Michael stood before responding, "Come in."

In walked Nadine, the red haired social worker that helped Michael navigate the last year of the emotionally draining case. Without her help, relating to Shamika would have been impossible.

"Thank goodness I made it in time. Traffic was ridiculous. You know what they say about Charlotte traffic, if you wanna make instant idiots just add water. I declare you'd think those people never seen rain before." Nadine wasted no time jumping directly into conversation, huffing and puffing as she limped into the room using her cane for support.

"Well hello to you too Nadine," Michael said as he moved to greet the older woman. "We're glad you made it in time." Michael leaned in and kissed Nadine on the cheek. The past year brought him closer to her than he was to his own mother, something neither of them saw coming.

"Hey Michael," Nadine said dismissively in her deep southern drawl. She cared for the young lawyer, but her focus was singular. She moved past Michael and walked over to the small table where Shamika sat staring down at nothing in particular. Nadine took a seat in the chair Michael first occupied. "Shamika, how are you?"

"I'm okay," Shamika whispered.

"What did I tell you about looking people in the eye when you speak?"

Shamika looked up into the clear blue eyes of the woman that had been more of a mother to her than her own mother had ever been. "I'm okay," she repeated.

"That's better. Remember something for me okay?"

Shamika nodded.

"No one on this earth is more important than you. What you have to say is valuable. You deserve the same respect everyone else receives. Okay?"

Shamika nodded once more.

"No one can hear you nod. Let your voice be heard."

"Yes Ma'am," Shamika replied.

A second knock on the door captured everyone's attention.

"Come on in," Michael yelled out.

A bailiff stuck his head in the door. "It's time," he said before pulling his head back out of view and closing the door.

Shamika's disposition immediately dropped and her eyes shifted back down towards the floor.

"Look at me," Nadine demanded.

Shamika obeyed.

"Hold your head up. You know the truth. The truth is what is going to make you free today. You hold on to that."

Nadine patted the top of Shamika's hand, stood, and moved towards the baby seat which still held the sleeping baby. She picked up the seat and started towards the door.

"Wait," Shamika yelled. She stood and rushed over to Nadine. "I need to hold him one last time, just in case… just in case they don't believe me."

Nadine walked to the table and placed the baby's seat on top of it. Shamika followed, unbuckled the straps, and removed her son. Baby Adrian squirmed a little, but did not wake. Shamika nestled her baby into her and walked over to the window as she whispered into his tiny little ear. She swayed and whispered until the bailiff knocked on the door again.

"I'm sorry Shamika, but we really have to get into the courtroom," Michael directed.

Shamika nodded and fought back tears. She walked back to the table where Nadine was still standing and placed her baby boy back into his seat. She took her time buckling him in and gave him a kiss on the forehead once the task was complete.

"I'm going to take him downstairs to the nursery and I'll come back up to hear the verdict. Remember what I said. What you have to say is just as valuable as everyone else. No matter what those jurors decide, you know the truth. Hold on to the truth Shamika, it's the one thing in life that never changes."

Without a word, Michael and Shamika left the room and headed down the hall to the courtroom. When they entered the room, the air was thick with tension. The gallery was full, a sign that the trial of a sixteen year old girl charged with first degree murder was considered interesting to a great number of people. There were several reporters ready to be the first to break the story. If convicted, Shamika faced life in prison without the possibility of parole. She would be the first teenager to receive the sentence since the U.S. Supreme Court ruled it constitutional for offenders age sixteen or older. Had Lamar attacked Shamika one day earlier when she was still fifteen, this would not be an issue. Offenders who were fifteen or younger could still face life in prison, but by law they would have to be given a possibility for parole. Lamar's terrible timing took that opportunity away from Shamika. Michael's only hope was that the jury could see the abuse Shamika suffered at the hands of her attacker and understand she acted in self-defense. She wasn't a calculating killer. She was a scared little girl fighting for her life. The past year of Michael's life built up to this moment. This case, this single case was the make or break case for him. Not just for his career, but for his life and the life of both Shamika and her baby.

1

Eleven months earlier...

"Yes! Yes! Yes," screamed the no name woman that Michael banged from behind. Of course she did have a name, but Michael had no clue what is was. All that mattered to him was the cute face, tight ass that looked yoga trained, and the tiny waist he now used to help him keep his balance. Stroke after stroke after stroke Michael pounded into her until he reached the climax he so desperately needed. Spent from his orgasm, Michael fell over on the bed and rolled onto his back. Sleeping with random women wasn't a favorite of his, but after the biggest win of his career he needed to celebrate. Successfully defending a Carolina Panthers player in the murder case of the century was sure to put him on the short list for partner at his father's firm Ayers, Rogers, & Winslow. At 34 years old, Michael planned to become the youngest partner since his father founded the firm twenty-five years ago. His most recent success was the feather in his hat.

"That smile on your face says I did my job well," the blonde said.

"You had a little to do with it, but this smile is work related. I just won a huge case today," Michael bragged.

"So, what are you, a cop or something?"

"A cop? Hell no! I'd never put my life on the line for $30,000 a year. No, I'm a defense attorney about to become partner at Charlotte's most prominent law firm."

"So if I ever get arrested, can I call you?"

"You could, but I can't promise I'd answer," Michael replied smugly before getting up to head into the bathroom, smacking her naked butt as he stood.

As soon as the bathroom door closed, the blonde hurriedly climbed out of the bed and rummaged through Michael's pockets. Once she found his wallet she retrieved three one hundred dollar bills and placed them on the nightstand. She grabbed her purse and retrieved the small bag of white powder. She placed the bag on the opposite nightstand. As she rushed to slip back into her panties and bra she picked up her cell phone and texted a single word, *now*.

Michael exited the bathroom to see her half-dressed and slipping into her shoes. Thank God I won't have to kick her out, he thought. I want this room to myself for the rest of the night.

"Leaving so soon?"

"Yeah, I have another…"

Her words were interrupted by a bang on the door.

"Police! Open up!"

"The police," Michael questioned. "What the hell are the police doing here?" Michael strode to the door wearing only his pants in his usual cavalier way. "Why the hell are you…"

"Get on the ground," the uniformed officer yelled as he pushed his way into the hotel room.

"Are you kidding me? Do you know who I am?"

"Yes, Michael. We know exactly who you are," Detective Jennings said with a smile as he entered the hotel room.

Michael threw his head back and laughed. "Detective Jennings, why am I not surprised you are behind this harassment?"

"Get on the ground," the uniformed officer yelled once more before drawing his gun and pointing it at Michael.

"Are you out of your mind? Tell him to stop pointing that thing at me," Michael yelled at Detective Jennings.

"I would suggest you follow his commands," Detective Jennings said with a smile.

"I'm not getting on the ground. I know my rights. I haven't done anything wrong. I'm going to have your fucking badge for this!"

"See Counselor, you're so cocky and you spend so much time flapping your gums that you miss the important details. Take for instance, the three hundred dollars laying there on the nightstand, the small bag of what appears to be cocaine on the opposite nightstand, and the half-dressed escort standing behind you."

Michael turned around and examined his surroundings. "Escort? You set me up!"

Detective Jennings laughed. "What's that saying you used in your closing this morning? Ah…yes, it's all coming back to me now. 'The law is all about tangible evidence.' Well in this case counselor, we have everything we need to arrest you on charges of solicitation and possession of a controlled substance. We'll have to test the baggie, but I'm pretty sure we both know what's in there."

Michael tried to lunge for Detective Jennings, but he was intercepted by the uniformed officer who had him on the ground with his hands behind his back before he knew what hit him. Yelling all types of obscenities at Detective Jennings, Michael allowed his body to go limp as the uniformed officer and his partner who was waiting in the hall, carried him out and placed him in the back of their squad car.

Sitting in the back of the squad car, Michael banged the back of his head against the seat. How could he be so stupid? How did he not realize the blonde was setting him up?

"Don't beat yourself up over this," Detective Jennings said from the front seat. "You've been so busy getting murderers out of prison lately that you forgot to watch your own back. It's cool though, I'm sure you'll find a way to lie your way out of this one too. Smile for the camera," Jennings said as he flashed a picture of Michael. "Oh and before I forget, the pro we caught you with is 17."

Vision blurry from the bright light of the camera's flash, Michael sat quietly stunned. The momentary lapse in sight was nothing compared to the tongue lashing he was about to hear from the old man. He wasn't worried about the charges. He knew he'd beat those. The real problem was his father.

Bruce Ayers, thirty years his senior never gave his son much slack. He raised Michael with meticulous rigor. He ensured his son went to all of the best schools and experienced the necessary cultural arts. Bruce worked around the clock, so the extent of his relationship with his son included teaching and molding Michael into becoming his successor. Michael banged his head once more and squeezed his eyes tightly at the thought of hearing one of his father's long drawn out lectures. All of the hard work he'd put into his last case would be forgotten and he didn't even get twenty-four hours to enjoy his victory.

***

Margaret Ayers sat across from her son in the sitting room while her husband Bruce raised holy hell about the evening's earlier events. She rolled her eyes around in her head as his sanctimonious speech continued to make her stomach curl. He seemed to have forgotten the mistakes of his youth and made Michael his personal pet project. His goal was to rush their son into taking over the firm, probably so he could go off and screw twenty something year old law students. Bruce foolishly believed Margaret didn't know about his indiscretions, but she had always known. In recent years she stopped looking and turned a blind eye, but she wasn't stupid, she knew he'd never stop.

"Mom!" Michael's voice brought Margaret back into the moment.

"There's no need to yell Dear. Despite your father's lectures my hearing remains intact."

"How can you sit here and let him say these things about me? You know I could never do what they are charging me with!"

Margaret stared blankly at her son while running her fingers across her pearls. She had no idea what her windbag husband said, but she did agree her son was no criminal. She'd raised him well. He was a member of one of the most elite families of Charlotte; he knew better than to muddy the family name with a scandal. "Yes, my darling. I know you are completely innocent. I'm sure your father will come to his senses shortly."

"Don't speak of me as though I am not standing right here," Bruce boomed. "You can't ignore cocaine and an underage hooker! This is your fault you know," he said waving his finger at Margaret. "You had one job! One job since the day I married you and that was to give me a son that I could trust to run my firm after I'm gone, and this is what I get? A drug user who sleeps with underage girls!"

"You will not speak to me this way," Margaret said with indignation as she rose to her feet. "If you took your nose from between the legs of young secretaries you'd realize there is no way my son could be guilty of what they are saying. My son, is nearly perfect in every way, his only flaw is your blood that runs through his veins. And since you want to talk about jobs, let's not forget it was my father's money and reputation that afforded you the opportunity to start your firm. So don't you look down your nose at me! Just do your job and make all of this go away. You're a defense attorney right? Defend him!" Margaret said with finality before storming out of the room. Her usually perfect dark brown hair was a long mass of curls bouncing behind her as she left.

Michael remained seated with his head in his hands. For some reason every time his parents fought, it turned him back into a ten year old boy. He couldn't speak to defend himself or look his father in the eye. No matter how unrealistic his desire, Michael still held out hope that his father would one day love him and respect the man he'd become. Sure he still made mistakes, but he was a damn good attorney and the old man knew that. He won more cases than any other junior associate. That fact alone should have won him the respect he deserved. He was the only child of the founding partner; in his opinion, he was entitled to become partner by default. The current criminal charges would make that task even more difficult to achieve.

Bruce sighed heavily, his grey eyes filled with concern. "I don't know how I'm going to fix this, but I will. However, you won't go unpunished. My silence in your upbringing is part of the reason you're such an arrogant jackass now."

"But Dad…"

"Don't but Dad me! I watch you. I see how you walk around with a superiority complex because you're the boss' son. That's my fault as well. I suppose I can't expect you to take responsibility for your actions if I don't do the same," Bruce said as his shoulders dropped. "I should have instilled values in you and helped you become a man, instead of a weak little boy trying to play dress up in Daddy's suits. Tonight is not only your failure, it's mine as well."

"Despite what you think, I am a man," Michael spewed angrily. "And I'm sick of trying to prove that to you," he said before getting up and storming out of the room.

"No son, you're not a man yet, but you will be by the time I finish with you," Bruce replied to an empty room.

***

"I'm fired?" Michael yelled at his father.

"Yes, go clean out your desk and don't make a scene. I don't need you creating early morning drama in the office."

"I can't believe you would fire your own son."

"Son, if I thought it would save you I'd cut off your left nut with a rusty knife."

"The rusty knife might cut less," Michael mumbled. "What am I supposed to do about money?"

"In exchange for making your charges go away I have arranged for you to do some community service work in the public defender's office. Since community service does not include a salary, you will work there for free and I will pay you a modest salary comparable to what the other lawyers in that office earn."

"What? You're actually serious? You are firing me and making me go work for lowlife criminals?"

"No, I'm going to make you work for the community. There are plenty of good people that can't afford a major firm like ours and you are going to go help them."

"How long are you going to make me stay there?"

"As long as it takes."

Michael turned to leave Bruce's office, but stopped to face him one final time. "My whole life I've been trying to get you to see me. It's a shame that the only time you actually do is when I get framed for a crime I didn't commit. Since starting law school I've tried to do everything exactly like you did. I requested to be placed on the most difficult cases and I have won more cases than any other junior associate here. I'm flawed, but I've worked my ass off."

Bruce took a long hard thought provoking breath. "No son. That's where you are wrong. You have won cases, but you and I both know you didn't win them due to your hard work. You cut corners and manipulate your way into winning. You use my name as leverage to get people to swing your way. You're nothing more than a common spoiled rich kid trying to make it on the back of his daddy's name," Bruce yelled more loudly than he intended to. The last few years of watching his arrogant child piss away a promising career were all coming back to him at once. "Just go clean out your office and leave before you cause an even bigger scene," he continued in a much softer tone.

"Fine, if this is what you want, but once I leave I'm not going to come back groveling for my old job. I'll find a firm that will understand and appreciate my talent, or maybe I'll start my own firm."

"Son, once you are released from community service, you can do whatever you like. Try to leave one second before I release you and I'll call the Charlotte Observer myself and have your arrest plastered all over the front page."

Adequate Counsel

2

Michael walked into the overly crowded stuffy building carrying a small cardboard box filled with his essentials. He didn't bother bringing all of his things because he didn't plan to stay very long. After thinking about the situation in the car ride over, Michael decided what he needed to do was start his own firm. He'd finish the community service and never look back at Ayers, Rogers, & Winslow. For now he'd tackle the first step which was community service in a building located not far from the courthouse that looked as though it was skipped during the recent "Keep Charlotte Beautiful" campaign.

Michael was raised in Ballantyne, one of the most affluent neighborhoods Charlotte, North Carolina had to offer. He attended Charlotte's most elite private schools until he graduated high school, afterwards attending the University of North Carolina at Chapel Hill for both undergrad and law school. He owned an upscale condo in downtown Charlotte complete with all of the amenities a man of his stature would enjoy, yet he rented an apartment in the only true high rise between New York and Miami. The condo was sufficient, but the apartment gave him views that left him speechless at night. A cleaning lady cleaned both homes three times a week and kept his fridge stocked with the essentials. He didn't even do his own laundry, and now here he stood in the dirtiest place he's ever been forced to visit. His shoulders dropped at the thought.

Michael wasn't in the building five minutes before his skin started to crawl. The narrow hallway was cluttered with plastic trees that looked as though they hadn't been dusted in years. There were benches occupied by people that looked as though they hadn't showered in years. Michael clutched his box and hastened his steps towards what appeared to be a receptionist desk. He approached the woman just as the phone on her desk began to ring. As was the custom at Ayers, Rogers, & Winslow, Michael expected the young woman to put her caller on hold and address his concern. He was shocked when she answered the phone and held a full conversation without acknowledging his presence. He stood there gaping at her until she ended her call.

"You just answered the phone and held a conversation after you saw me approach you."

"And?"

"And? What do you mean and?"

"And what is your point," the woman said adding a distinct neck roll to the question.

"My point is that it is extremely rude to ignore someone that is standing right in front of your face! Especially a new attorney your firm is trying to impress."

The woman threw her head back in laughter. "Look Sugah, I don't know where you think you are, but this here ain't nobody's firm. This is a legal office for folks that can't afford stuffy uptight high priced lawyers. And my job ain't to impress nobody. Now if you don't like what you see, turn around and take your narrow white ass right back out that door."

"Are you kidding me? You actually speak to people this way? Do you have any idea who I am?"

"No, and I don't give a hot damn," the woman said louder than Michael expected.

"You should be fired! This is an outrage," Michael yelled as he threw his box down on her desk.

The woman narrowed her eyes as she slid her chair back from beneath the desk. She stood up and walked around to stand toe to toe with Michael. With her standing immediately in front of him Michael noticed a few things about this woman. Not only did she stand at least three inches above his five foot ten frame, but her face looked as though she'd lived a rough life. Her make-up helped to conceal some of the scars, but up close Michael could see the woman had multiple blemishes that looked like old cuts on her cheeks. She had breasts that looked like they led her around and hands that could probably palm a basketball. In a word, the woman was…scary. Michael tried to take a step back after seeing that he was physically outmatched. The woman closed the space between them by stepping forward.

"That's enough Tanya," a voice called from behind Michael. "Don't scare the man away on his first day."

The woman, now identified as Tanya smiled down at Michael. "You better be happy Mr. Willoughby showed up or I would have kicked your lily white ass all over this place," she whispered.

More confident now that he knew he was safe, Michael returned her smile. "Good, I like it rough," he said with a wink before picking up his box and turning to face his new boss.

"Mr. Willoughby, it's a pleasure to finally meet you," Michael said turning on the charm.

Mr. Willoughby waited until they were safely out of the reception area before responding. As they walked down another long dark hallway, he began to give Michael the ground rules. "You can cut the act. You and I both know you don't want to be here. Truth be told, I don't want you here, but I owe your father a favor so we're stuck dealing with each other until you get your act together."

"Until I get my…"

Mr. Willoughby stopped in his tracks causing Michael to nearly bump into him. He turned to look Michael in the eye, "Rule number one, never interrupt me when I'm talking. Over at your father's firm your name carries weight, here you're at the bottom of my shit list just like every other pompous young lawyer that walks through those doors. Your work ethic is terrible and I could run circles around you with my knowledge of the very thing you think you know so much about. When I speak I give out information you will one day be able to use, so stop yapping and listen. Do we understand each other?"

Michael stared at the tall balding black man who even through his suit appeared to be in wonderful shape. He stood at least four or five inches over Michael and his eyes held a unique austerity. Thomas Willoughby was known for his no nonsense attitude, but of course Michael never experienced it firsthand until now. He had a reputation of whipping lawyers into shape. Michael knew exactly why his father sent him to work for Thomas, but had no intentions of allowing anyone to "break" him. He'd do his time and get the hell out of dodge. Still unsure how they could have a mutual understanding when only one of them had been given the opportunity to speak, Michael simply nodded his head in the affirmative.

Mr. Willoughby turned and walked a few steps in silence. When he stopped he turned and opened a door. He stepped to the side and motioned for Michael to go before him. Michael walked into the tiny room with no window and cringed.

"This will be your office. How long you stay here is up to you. Everyone here is expected to give our clients the best possible defense. We have a shoestring budget and our caseloads are too heavy. We work long hours and if we do happen to get a break, it's a very short one. I expect you to arrive no later than 7:30 am every morning, and unless you are in court I expect you to be here combing through your files and creating a useable defense. In this office we can't turn away cases. We defend everyone that can't afford counsel, and we do it well. If you don't like the client, learn how to fake it. I won't have my reputation ruined with inadequate counsel rulings," Mr. Willoughby paused for effect and looked over the rim of his large round glasses to be sure Michael understood his last point before continuing. "You'll be assigned cases as they come in. We have a morning meeting in about half an hour. You'll get your first cases at that time. Do you have any questions?"

Michael's head was swimming, but he simply shook his head no.

"Great, I'll have someone come grab you in a little while. For now get settled. This is the most downtime you'll have while working here," Mr. Willoughby said before leaving the office and closing the door behind him.

Michael sat his box down on the small wooden desk. He looked around at the small closet someone previously decided to turn into an office. In addition to the desk the furnishings in the room included two chairs; one for him, and one apparently for clients; a wastebasket; and a tall narrow shelf that would never be able to hold all of his law books. Michael walked around the desk to get a better look at its storage capacity. As he suspected two things became very evident; had the shelf been two inches wider he would not have been able to squeeze between it and the desk, and the three drawers in the desk were not even big enough to hold the contents of his box.

Michael took a seat behind the desk. The chair creaked as he plopped his weight into it. He leaned forward, propped his elbows on the desk and buried his face into his hands. His thoughts went into overdrive as the recent events replayed in his mind. Just a few days prior he was at the top of his game, rushing to become the youngest partner in the history of the firm. He won the biggest case of his career, a national football player with very incriminating evidence. He actually pulled off the win no one thought he'd be able to pull off. He'd won the firm's highest profile case in years, and one stupid act of picking up a random blonde at the bar landed him in the hell hole his father decided would be best for him. He knew Detective Jennings had it out for him ever since he humiliated him on the stand, but he never thought the man would set him up. Now that he didn't have the high power resources of his father's firm, he would need favors to win cases. He'd always had access to money, never once had he called in a favor. He wasn't even sure he'd made any friends that would do favors for him. The entire way he practiced law was potentially in danger.

"How the hell am I supposed to work under these conditions?"

"The same way the rest of us do," a female voice said startling him.

Michael was so engrossed in thought, he didn't hear anyone enter the room. He looked up and opened his mouth to speak, but snatched it shut. At least ten years had passed, but she was still as beautiful as the day they met. Her long blonde tresses were a few inches shorter than he remembered, but the cut made her even more stunning. Michael's eyes roamed down the body of the woman in front of him. Her physique was slightly hidden by the dark suit she wore, but he could tell even through her clothing that she remained as fit as he remembered. He wondered if she still played tennis five days a week. As his eyes traveled back up he noticed her left hand was void of jewelry, a thought that made him feel unexplainably warm inside. His eyes continued their route until he locked in on her big beautiful brown eyes. She was in every way still the perfect specimen of woman. He finally smiled at her.

"Kate! What are you doing here?"

"I work here," she said returning his smile and walking further into the office to take the seat opposite of him. "The question is what the hell are you doing here? Everyone knows you are the son of the most successful defense attorney in Charlotte, hell arguably the whole state of North Carolina. What are you doing slumming down here with the rest of us mere mortals?"

Michael absorbed her accent. Her light Carolinian twang always sounded like music to his ears. "Let's just say my father hasn't changed much since you saw him last," Michael said with a sigh. "He still thinks I'm five and waiting for him to come home and teach me some sort of lesson."

"After your big win I'd say Daddy's lessons must have been pretty darn good."

"So you know about that huh? Have you been reading up on me over the years?" Michael smiled like a kid back in high school at the thought of Kate following his career for the last few years.

Kate rolled her eyes. "Don't flatter yourself Egoman. Everyone knew about that case. There were reporters all over the city for months because of it."

"I guess you're right. You can't blame a guy for holding out hope though can you?" He flashed his brilliantly white slightly crooked smile. It made women melt every time. In fact, it was the same smile that won Kate over back in college.

"Stay on topic here Counselor. What are you doing here?"

"Like you already mentioned, I learned from the best."

"What does that mean?"

"My father's lessons are part of the reason I'm out of his good graces at the moment."

She furrowed her brow.

"Let's just say monkey see monkey do is what got me into this mess."

"I have no idea what you are talking about, but we better head on up to the meeting or Thomas is going to have your head," she said as she rose to her feet.

Michael followed suit and stood as well. "So you get to call old Willoughby by his first name huh? What did you have to do to earn that honor," he asked teasingly as he followed her out of the office and towards the elevators he'd passed earlier on his way in.

She stopped and pressed the up button on the wall before turning to face him. "When your win rate is as high as mine, you call the boss whatever you want," she said with a wink just as the elevator dinged.

Once inside she pushed the button for the tenth floor. Michael did his best not to stare, but her beauty was a sight to behold.

"Stop looking at me like that," she demanded without looking in his direction.

"You're not even looking at me, how do you know how I'm looking at you?"

"Because I know you Mike."

"You haven't seen me in ten years. You don't know me like you think you do."

"I know enough," she said still not looking in his direction.

As the elevator doors opened so did Michael's mind to the gravity of his situation. Not only was the suite of offices clean and well lit, the space was huge and inviting. The tenth floor was in direct contrast to the bottom level Michael was assigned to. His face twisted in anger as he looked around the space at the smiling faces of the well-dressed attorneys and paralegals. The office walls were mostly made of glass giving Michael full visual access to the well decorated offices. Many of the exterior walls held large picture windows with breathtaking views of the Charlotte Skyline. The space was beautiful. Michael's skin flushed and his face twisted. He grabbed Kate's arm and pulled her closer to him.

"That son of a bitch stuck me in the dungeon and the rest of you work up here? Does he really think he can do this to me," he whispered angrily.

Kate pulled her arm from his grasp. "Newsflash Trust Fund baby, this is not Ayers, Rogers, & Winslow.

Around here everyone works their way from the bottom up," she said harshly before turning and rushing away from him.

"Shit," Michael cursed under his breath before hurrying behind her.

"Kate! Kate! Kate, wait slow down," Michael called as he tried to catch up with her. Just as she reached her destination, Michael reached out to grab her again, but missed as she entered the office on their right. "Dammit Kate," Michael yelled just as he walked into an office full of watchful eyes.

"Ah Mr. Ayers, it's nice to see you have found your way to our morning meeting," Mr. Willoughby announced.

Michael hung his head and cursed under his breath once more.

"Uh, hi Mr. Willoughby. Kate was an excellent guide," Michael stammered under everyone's gaze as he made his way to an open chair in the back of the room.

"Now that everyone is here," Thomas said clearing his throat, "let's get started, shall we?"

"Wait," said a young man sitting close to the front of the room. "Aren't you going to introduce the newest member of the team?"

"No," replied Thomas with finality. "This is not social hour. And with your current losing streak I would suggest you focus on your cases, not your colleagues."

The young man lowered his eyes before making eye contact with Michael. Knowing he wasn't the only one Thomas treated with disdain brought a level of comfort to Michael. Maybe the old man didn't hate him after all. That thought gave him hope.

After more than an hour of listening to everyone review their cases the meeting was dismissed and everyone began filing out of the room quickly. Seeing attorneys move with such haste was not common for Michael, but he attempted to join in. He grabbed his notepad and stood to leave the room.

"Mr. Ayers," called Thomas. "Follow me. We have some cases to discuss."

Michael tucked his notepad under his arm and followed Thomas into an office that rivaled those he was accustomed to. He tried not to become angry at the difference between Thomas' office and the closet he'd been given but his face didn't cooperate.

"I know what you're thinking," Thomas said as he took his seat behind his rich mahogany desk.

Michael remained silent.

"Have a seat," Thomas said gesturing to one of the wing back chairs that faced his desk.

Michael complied.

"You're thinking I'm about to hand you a tough case load full of impossible cases."

Again Michael remained silent, but tried to soften his expression. His efforts were futile.

"Well Mr. Ayers, you're wrong, so you can wipe that sour look off of your face. I'm going to start you the same way I start everyone else. Here are your cases," Thomas said as he pushed a large stack of manila folders in Michael's direction.

Michael leaned forward and grabbed the first file. He opened the folder, skimmed the first couple of pages, and pushed the folder aside. He repeated the process until he'd gone through the entire stack of folders. Once complete he sat back in bewilderment.

"They're kids. Every last one of them."

"Yes, Michael they are. Do you have a problem with that?"

"Uh...yeah. As a matter of fact I do. What am I supposed to do with children?"

"You can start by defending them."

"Defending them? Why are their files even here? Don't they have a juvenile court system for this stuff?"

Thomas rolled his eyes and ran his hand over the stubble that covered the top of his head. "Please don't tell me that your head is so far up your rich ass that you didn't know this office handles cases in the juvenile system."

Michael's face twisted at the insult. "Excuse me for working too hard to stay abreast on the inner workings of legal aid," he said in a tone that let Thomas know exactly what he thought about the office.

"Listen here you little shit. I don't tolerate that type of attitude from anyone, but especially not a spoiled little boy that can't keep his hands off of teenage girls. You should be behind bars, but because of your daddy's reputation I'm stuck babysitting you. Now I agreed to let you serve your community service here, but with that agreement comes a requirement for you to do as you are told. You lost your ability to act all high and mighty when you were caught with a seventeen year old. Now take those files and get the hell out of my office!"

Michael stood quickly and yelled, "Screw you and those files. I don't need this shit!" He stormed out of Thomas' office and headed straight for the elevators.

He wasn't going to sit there and allow anyone to talk to him like he didn't matter. Despite Detective Jennings' efforts, Michael knew he wasn't any of the things people were believing him to be. When the elevator dinged he hurried inside and pushed the button for the first floor. He stood fuming as he waited to reach the bottom floor. As soon as the elevator doors opened, Michael rushed back to the tiny closet-like office he'd been assigned. He grabbed his box and headed towards the front door. He wasn't going to spend another minute in the disgusting building. When he reached the door that led to the lobby he sucked his teeth at the sight of Tanya, the rude gatekeeper that made his first impression of the building line up with his last impression. They were all a bunch of insolent SOBs and he wouldn't tolerate their disrespect.

As he rushed pass Tanya he heard her yell out, "So you're gone already, huh? That's a record." But he kept walking. He had nothing to say to her. Michael reached his car, popped the trunk and angrily threw his box inside. He slammed the trunk shut and rushed to get inside. He needed to put some distance between himself and the building his father thought would make an appropriate place for him to serve his sentence. Michael started his engine and sped away from the building thinking how ironic his father's actions were. They were both defense lawyers. They both dedicated their lives to finding ways to help their clients reach not guilty verdicts, yet now that Michael was framed, his father didn't even try to help him. Bruce Ayers made himself judge and sentenced his son without giving Michael a chance to defend himself. He gripped the steering wheel tighter as he thought of it all. He zoomed in and out of traffic barely focusing on the road. The sound of his ringing cell phone brought him back to himself. He pressed the answer button located on his steering wheel without bothering to look at the console to see who was calling.

"Hello," he growled.

"Michael, what the hell did you just do?" Bruce Ayers' voice boomed through the car's speakers.

"What do you mean what did I do? What did you do sending your only son to that filthy place to be treated like shit?"

"I told you to go down there and do community service. I didn't tell you to go make friends or relax in luxury. Now turn your spoiled ass around and go back this instant or I'm calling the Observer."

"You wouldn't risk ruining your only son and there's no way Mom will let you leak a scandal about me, so stop with the idle threats."

"Idle threats? You disrespectful…"

Michael ended the call before his father could finish his sentence. "If you want to destroy me old man, go ahead and try. I'm sick of this shit."

3

"Another round Bartender," Michael slurred from the stool he'd been perched on for more than four hours. "How do you expect me to get drunk with you moving so slow?"

"It looks like you managed that hours ago," the sultry bartender replied.

Michael smiled. "Ah, so you've been watching me as hard as I've been watching you," he said with flirtation dripping heavily through his words.

"Of course. I notice all of the handsome men that come in and look like they can leave me big tips."

"See, now that wounded me," Michael said grabbing his chest and feigning pain. "Here I was thinking you were after me for my intellect and you were only thinking about my wallet."

The bartender smiled as she sat the fresh drink in front of Michael. "I'm working. I have to think about your wallet."

Michael grabbed her arm. "After work will you think about something else? I have something in my pants that's way more interesting than my wallet."

The bartender's eyes widened at Michael's suggestion. She tried to pull away, but he held on to her arm.

"Come back to my place. It's not far from here. Let me take your mind off of work."

"If you do not release my arm, I will break your wrist," the bartender said with confidence.

"She likes it rough," Michael teased with lust glistening in his eyes.

"This is your last warning, Buddy. Let me go or I will break your shit off," she said loud enough for the other patrons to hear. Heads turned in their direction, but drunken Michael didn't bother to obey her command. Within seconds, the bartender used her free hand to remove Michael's grip and twist his hand into some sort of submission hold.

"Aaaaagghhhh," Michael screamed out in pain.

"I warned you, didn't I?" the pissed off bartender yelled in the face of a pained Michael.

"Okay, that's enough. Let him go," a familiar female voice called out.

The bartender looked up at Kate who was now moving in their direction. She released Michael while speaking to Kate. "You better get this son of a bitch out of here before he makes me permanently disable that arm."

Michael looked up to see Kate staring at him with pure anger in her eyes. Her presence helped to sober him slightly. "What the hell are you doing here?"

"Don't worry about why I'm here, just be glad I saved your ass," Kate replied curtly. "Now pay your tab so we can leave, and give Megan here a big tip to apologize for the way you behaved."

"I'm not giving her a tip. She just assaulted me," Michael fussed as he fished into his wallet for cash.

Kate snatched the wallet, found two crisp one hundred dollar bills and placed them on the counter in front of Megan the bartender. "Here you go Megan, please forgive my drunken colleague. He's almost house trained when he's sober."

Michael gaped at Kate before responding. "You just gave her two hundred dollars? She tried to break my wrist," he protested.

"It was your fault for grabbing her arm, now come on so I can get you home. I have an early hearing in the morning so I need to get some rest."

Michael stood and nearly lost his balance. Kate grabbed him and wrapped his right arm around her neck, making him suppress a smile. She helped him keep his balance as they walked out of the bar. As they stepped out into the night air, she stopped. "Which way?"

"This way," Michael replied turning to the left. They walked in silence for two blocks before Kate dared to speak again mostly due to the unpleasant smell of brown liquor on Michael's breath.

"What's the name of your building?"

"The Vue," he responded blowing his breath directly into Kate's face. If she wasn't sure her feelings for him were long gone, this night was erasing any fantasy she ever held.

"Good. We're almost there," Kate said starting to feel the pressure of supporting his weight on her shoulders.

When they reached the building, Michael attempted to find his key card to enter, but the concierge buzzed him in on sight. "Good evening Mr. Ayers," the concierge greeted him kindly as they entered the building.

I wonder how often he staggers in like this, Kate thought to herself.

Michael did not bother to respond. He simply headed for the elevators and stood waiting as if he could will the doors to open. Kate rolled her eyes as she leaned forward and pushed the call button on the wall. The elevator opened immediately allowing them to enter.

"Which floor?"

"49," Michael replied.

Kate hid her amazement as she pressed the appropriate button. She knew Michael probably lived in some overpriced building, but the forty ninth floor in Charlotte's premiere high rise was not what she had in mind. She wasn't sure why she was surprised though. Michael's father was the most successful defense attorney in the city, arguably the state and his mother's family had more money than they knew what to do with. It only made sense for him to throw away seven thousand dollars a month on an apartment. Still, the waste of it all saddened her. The Michael she thought she knew in college was a jerk, but he wasn't this pompous, arrogant, money wasting drunk that currently leaned on her for support. She wanted to ask him how he allowed himself to become the one person he said he never wanted to be, but she decided against it.

The elevator door dinged and they exited. Kate followed Michael's lead and turned right. When they reached his door, Michael fished his keys out with ease and opened the door. He removed his arm from Kate's shoulder and walked inside.

"So all of a sudden you're sober?" Kate yelled as she walked in behind him.

"I'm not sober, but I'm not as drunk as you believed," Michael said with a smile.

"Then why did you almost turn me into a hunch back walking you home?"

"How else would I have gotten you to come home with me?"

Kate's blood rushed to her face. "I should have let Megan kick your ass. I can't believe I fell for this shit!" Kate turned to storm out of the apartment, but Michael ran and grabbed her hand.

"Kate, please I'm sorry. You're right I am an asshole, but please don't leave. Stay for just a little while. I promise I'll be on my best behavior."

Kate listened to his plea and narrowed her eyes. "Why should I believe anything that comes out of that lying hole in your face?"

Michael released her hand and took a deep breath once again blowing his liquor laden breath in her face.

Kate flinched.

Michael covered his mouth in embarrassment. "I'm sorry," he mumbled with his hand still covering his mouth. He took a step back before dropping his hand and speaking. "Please Kate. I know I'm a fool and I shouldn't have tricked you, but I could really use a friend right now. I saw you watching me at the bar. I know I should have just went over and spoke to you, but I didn't want a public conversation. I want what we used to have, you know back in college. Sitting up all night talking about life. No one has ever helped me clear my head like you used to. I know you don't have all night, but just a little while. Please, just give me a minute to freshen up and I promise to be the perfect gentleman.

Kate's shoulders relaxed and against her better judgment she agreed to stay.

Michael smiled his second genuine smile of the day. "Come on over here and make yourself comfortable," he said motioning towards the living area.

Kate obliged and plopped down on his soft leather sofa. Michael disappeared into the back of the apartment while Kate relaxed. She took in the surroundings of the apartment. Every inch looked like it had been designed by a professional. No man Kate knew could put together a room so well balanced. Besides, she doubted Michael had the patience or mental capacity required for decorating anything. Kate stood and moved towards the large windows. The view of Charlotte was breath taking. She stood soaking up the skyline and thinking of how boring her life in her tiny house in South Charlotte was compared to Michael's life here in the heart of the city.

"That's my favorite thinking spot," Michael said startling her.

Kate jumped slightly and turned to the sound of his voice. Her breath caught again, but this time it wasn't due to being startled. Michael stood a few feet away from her wearing what appeared to be pajama bottoms and a black ribbed tank. Without the barrier of his suit, Kate enjoyed a view of the biceps she once held onto for support when he made love to her. Though she didn't plan to, her mind flashed back to the nights of passion they shared in law school. Her body instantly ached to be touched by him again. She licked her now dry lips and tried to look away. Before succeeding her eyes betrayed her and darted to his crotch. If memory was serving her correctly, and she was sure it was, the bulge in his pants wasn't indicative of all he had to offer. The man made her experience things in bed she never thought she could.

She'd had a boyfriend or two since him, but no one held a candle to his skill in the bedroom.

"Get a grip Kate," she inwardly admonished herself as she turned around to stare out of the window once more. She needed to look at something, anything other than the beautiful man standing behind her. Even while looking away, she knew he was still staring at her. The moisture developing between her thighs told her he was still staring and thinking about the same thing she was thinking about. She needed to destroy the sexual tension in the air before she did something she would regret. Michael was an ex for a reason, she needed to remind herself of that. He wasn't marriage material.

"So, how long have you lived here?" She asked the question casually hoping her voice was steady.

"A little over a year," he said as he stepped closer to her.

Kate closed her eyes and tightened her body. She silently prayed he wouldn't touch her. She knew she would lose control if she felt those strong hands slide around her waist like they did in college.

"The view is stunning. It would have made me move here as well," she said without opening her eyes.

"How can you see the view with your eyes closed," he said in a low sexy tone that only heightened her libido.

Kate opened her eyes to see Michael standing next to her staring into her face intently. "I stared at it for a while. I closed my eyes for a second."

Michael smiled. Kate looked away and willed her heart to stop racing.

"Would you like to sit out on the balcony?"

"I really shouldn't," Kate protested. "I have to be in court very early tomorrow morning. You've already tricked me into walking you home. I need to get back to my car and get going. Shit!" she exclaimed at the thought of her car.

Michael smiled. "I was wondering how long it was going to take you to figure that out."

Kate fumed as she turned to look at him. "Michael you are a selfish asshole! How could you trick me into walking you here? You knew it wouldn't be safe for me to walk back alone at this hour!" All sexual attraction to the man standing in front of her vanished. Her inner thoughts were correct. He was still the same arrogant selfish asshole he was in college.

"Calm down, I can have a car service take you home."

"How am I supposed to get to work tomorrow? Everyone doesn't have the luxury of just dialing up a car service."

"Relax, they can take you back to your car tonight, or I'll pay them to drive you around tonight and during the day tomorrow. You can pick your car up after work."

"No thank you. I'll go get my car tonight. The next time I see you about to get your ass kicked, I'm going to let the girl beat the shit out of you." Kate turned and headed for the door.

"Hey. Wait. Hold up," Michael walked behind her and caught her arm.

As Kate turned she pulled her arm from his grasp, raised her hand, and slapped Michael hard on the cheek. He released her and placed his hand over his stinging face.

"What was that for?"

"That was for tricking me into feeling sorry for you."

"Bullshit."

Kate stepped back and looked at him incredulously.

"Don't give me that look. We both know that slap had ten years of sting on it. You're still pissed about college."

"Don't flatter yourself Michael. I haven't thought about you in years."

"Don't lie to yourself. You were never really good at pretending. You were turned on the minute I walked back in here. And don't try to deny it. If I rip your panties off right now I'm sure there's a flood waiting for me."

"Fuck you," Kate said as she opened the door and rushed out of the apartment.

"Kate! Wait. Dammit, I've been chasing behind you all day."

"Then maybe you should keep your foot out of your mouth," she said without slowing down.

"Okay, okay. I'm sorry," he said when he caught up with her in front of the elevator. "This has been one of the roughest days of my life. I've been set up for something I didn't do, my father fired me, I got sent to a closet at the office while everyone else is living it up, and the woman that got away from me ten years ago suddenly pops up. I've looked for you over the years and could never find you then today of all days you show up twice. Any man would be an asshole right now. The stress of all of this is killing me. I'm sorry. I shouldn't have taken it out on you. Can you just give me a second chance to make a second impression? I meant what I said earlier...I need you Kate."

The wounded sound in his voice made her soften despite her better judgment. She wanted to remain cold and mean. She needed a buffer between the two of them, but she found her resolve slipping as she silently turned and headed back towards his apartment. Michael followed her and rested his head on the door when they were safely back inside. Kate, as if drawn by some unknown force, instantly went back to the window.

"Would you like a cup of coffee?"

"Sure," she replied still staring out of the window.

"I'll grab the coffee. Why don't you head on out to the balcony. There are blankets in the storage bin underneath the seat cushions. Grab a couple for us and I'll be right out with the coffee."

Kate followed his instructions. She wasn't settled long before he joined her. He handed her the coffee mug and they both sat in companionable silence for a while. The sounds of the night lulled them both and reduced the previous tension.

"What were you accused of doing?"

Michael looked into his mug as though it contained all of the answers. He hesitated before responding.

"I'd really rather not talk about it. Just know I didn't do it."

Kate nodded still able to hear the pain in his voice. She decided not to pressure him. She liked calm and relaxed Michael. He reminded her of the man she once loved.

"Tell me about you. What have you been up to these last ten years?"

Kate nervously tucked her hair behind her ear. "There's not much to tell really. I graduated law school and contemplated moving back home to Charleston, but I was offered the position in the public defender's office and it seemed like an opportunity to do something meaningful with my degree."

"You were at the top of our class. You could have easily gotten a job at a prestigious firm. Why settle for defending lowlifes?" As soon as the words left Michael's lips he regretted them.

Kate took a deep breath. "I wouldn't expect you to understand, but not everyone that comes through our office falls into the lowlife category. I've met some pretty amazing people that for whatever reason found themselves on the wrong side of the law. Some have been guilty. Some weren't, but that's not what matters. What matters is that everyone is entitled to adequate counsel. Our justice system tends to honor the constitutional rights of those that can afford high priced lawyers while the underprivileged are forced to accept what they can get. That just feels wrong to me, you know? I accepted the job with the intent of balancing the scales."

"Are we talking scales of justice or socioeconomic scales?"

"Both," Kate replied as she stared off into the Charlotte skyline. Michael watched as her eyes lightly glossed over. He waited while she enjoyed the moment she was experiencing. He loved watching her. She seemed to display all of her thoughts and feelings on her face.

"Tell me about it," he urged.

"About what?" Kate asked with a hesitant giggle.

"The memory that just took you away from me."

Kate looked down into her mug and then back out into the night. She held her breath for a moment before speaking.

"It was Davion."

"Wait, I don't want to hear about some man that broke your heart."

Kate didn't bother to acknowledge his comment. "I'd only been working in the office for about two months. I was tired, over worked, and underpaid. I was young and inexperienced. I didn't understand the magnitude of the cases. I thought I did, but I really didn't. Anyway, one morning Thomas comes into my office and tells me he needs me to take a case involving a fifteen year old facing attempted murder charges. I go interview the boy, meet with the mother, and review the file and it seems like an open and shut case. Davion confessed to shooting the mother's boyfriend because he didn't like him. The prosecutor offered a plea deal. Davion would plead guilty and serve a lesser sentence of ten years. I took the offer to my client and his mother, and they both agreed he would take the deal. I felt like it was an open and shut case. I was wrong."

Kate held her head down for a moment. Despite the darkness of the evening, Michael caught a glimpse of the tears that rolled down her cheek. He remained silent as she weighed through the emotions inside of herself. He wanted to reach out and hold her, but knew he needed to refrain. After a few moments she spoke once more.

"A month after the conviction, I'm sitting at home watching the news and the mother's face flashes across the screen. All I could do was watch in horror as the news caster told the story. The boyfriend killed the mother and her two daughters before fatally shooting himself. He'd only been out of the hospital for two weeks."

Kate paused again to wipe away her tears.

"You couldn't have known," Michael said trying to reassure her.

"I should have known! That son of bitch had been beating that woman for years. I should have investigated the family! I should have asked the right questions instead of accepting the bogus confession. I should have seen the signs of distress in the mother. I should have caught it all," she said as her voice trailed off.

"You couldn't have known. You were young and inexperienced."

"That's not an excuse when someone's life is on the line! When I graduated law school and decided to become a defense attorney, I wasn't ready for all this position would mean. We're not talking about minor offenses here; the boy went to prison at fifteen! That was on me because I wasn't efficient or experienced enough to defend him properly."

"You can't put all of that on your shoulders. Thomas obviously thought you were capable because he assigned the case to you."

"Well I did. And Thomas doesn't know everything," Kate snapped.

Michael weighed his next question carefully, but decided to ask it anyway. "What happened to your client?"

"I worked like hell for seven months straight, but I got his conviction overturned. I did everything I could to help him, but he never recovered from the loss of his mother and sisters. I think prison actually turned him into a criminal. He had never been in trouble before the shooting, yet he was killed in a botched robbery less than a year later."

"Damn," Michael said with a sigh. "It wasn't your fault."

"In my head I know that, but in my heart I wonder what would have happened if I would have dug deeper while the boyfriend was still in the hospital. I wonder if I would have been able to get the charges against my client dropped and gotten that asshole locked up. My head knows it's not my fault, but my heart remembers the pain and failure I felt when I learned the whole story. That case changed me. I became all about the client. Innocent or guilty; black, white, or other; young or old; male or female; rich or poor, I give them the defense they deserve."

4

Michael squinted at the sunlight that peeked through the windows. He felt the weight of another person lying next to him and smiled as he looked down at Kate. She was beautiful as her hair cascaded down her face. He propped himself up on one hand to get a better view of the sleeping beauty. After a few moments she began to stir under his gaze as if she knew she was being watched. She opened her eyes, appeared startled for a moment, and then sat up without returning his smile.

"You were supposed to stay on the couch."

"I did for most of the night, but I have a bad back," Michael lied.

"No you don't. You just wanted to trick me into getting in bed with you. Suckering me into walking you home wasn't enough?"

Michael smiled in that twisted way that Kate always loved. She told her heart to slow its beating once more as she left the bed and headed for the bathroom. When she returned Michael was sitting up with his back against the headboard and his bare chest in full view. His muscles reminded her of why she needed to get out of his apartment as soon as possible.

"Can you have a driver come and take me to my car? I need to get home as soon as possible so I can make it to court on time."

"I'll take you."

"What? You have a car?"

"Of course I have a car. You think I'm so out of touch that someone has to drive me everywhere?" Michael continued smiling and toying with her as he put on his shirt and shoes.

"If you have a car, why didn't you take me to mine last night?"

Michael walked close to her. So close, she feared he may kiss her. With her hormones raging from the months she'd been dry, plus the memories of his expert lovemaking, she knew a kiss would be her undoing. Yet she stood there with his nose so close to her face that she could smell the aftershave on him and tell he'd been awake much longer than she had. He leaned in and placed his left hand on her hip while kissing her on the forehead.

"I wanted to have you in my bed again," he whispered before releasing her and walking out of the room.

Kate released the breath she didn't know she'd been holding. She dropped her head before following him out of the bedroom.

***

"You decided to come back, huh?" Kate asked as she peeped into Michael's office.

He put down the file he'd been studying and looked up at her. His heart did that weird thing it always does when she comes around, but he tried to keep his tone even.

"Yeah, I decided to give it a shot."

"What made you change your mind?"

"A certain beautiful woman with a passion for justice for all," Michael said with a smile.

Kate's cheery expression faded. She walked into his office and shut the door behind her. The small room seemed even more cramped with the door closed, but Michael tried to ignore the feeling of claustrophobia and focus on Kate.

"I have something I need to tell you. I should have said something last night, but for whatever reason I didn't," Kate said as she wrung her hands and looked at the floor. "At first I was upset with you for being the arrogant social elitist I met in college, but after talking to you, I remembered the things about you that attracted me to you ten years ago."

"That's a good thing," Michael interrupted.

"No, it's not. I'm seeing someone and I can't let myself be sucked into the what-ifs of an old relationship. I'll help you here at work any way I can, but there won't be any more interaction between us outside of work."

Michael shrugged and chuckled a bit. "Kate, you're acting like we slept together. We talked and you left. It was no big deal."

"It may not have been a big deal to you, but it was to me, so it can't happen again okay?" Kate turned and opened the door to leave. When she did, she walked right into the chest of Thomas Willoughby. "Oh my goodness, I'm so sorry," she stammered before rushing down the hall.

Thomas shook his head in confusion as he walked into Michael's office. He shut the door behind him just as Kate did. Michael stood to shake Thomas' hand, but Thomas refused.

"Have a seat Michael. All that formality isn't necessary."

Michael did as instructed.

"I want to be very clear with you," Thomas began. "I'm going to excuse your little tantrum yesterday because I can imagine this is a difficult time for you, but I do not allow slackers to work in this office. Bottle up that personal bullshit and leave it in the car until after the work day is over. Understand?"

Michael nodded his head.

"Now, I also don't know what is going on between you and Kate, but there is absolutely no time for any interoffice romance here. Keep it strictly professional and focus on the needs of the clients. Study their cases, give them a proper defense. That's why you're here, not to distract my employees. Got it?"

Michael nodded his head once more.

"Now, I hope you are a fast reader because you are due in court for a bail hearing in an hour."

"What? Which case?"

"Mr. Ayers, it isn't my job to spoon feed you everything. Find the board, find the name, find the file, make it to court on time, and serve the client. That's your job," Thomas said as he stood and left the office.

Michael rushed about solving the riddle of his pending court appearance, which he quickly learned included more than just one bail hearing. Multiple cases assigned to him were on the docket for the day. He grabbed his briefcase, stuffed the related files inside and made the short walk to the courthouse. Though he'd practiced law in this city for years, he'd never walked to the courthouse. Working downtown in his new dingy office was a far cry from the South Park suite of offices Ayers, Rogers, & Winslow occupied. His brief walk afforded him a moment to think and absorb the surroundings of a city he previously thought he knew everything about.

After making it to the first courtroom, Michael took a seat in the gallery instead of in the area designated for attorneys. He wanted to just take a moment to witness the justice system at work from a different perspective. There weren't very many people around him, a fact that led Michael to believe those that were there were defendants waiting to hear their name be called. He tried to inconspicuously examine everyone and guess what their charges were but as name after name was called, he was wrong.

After two hours of watching and listening to the hushed conversations of those around him, Michael stood and walked to the appropriate space in the courtroom. He took a seat next to an unfamiliar attorney and began to read over the file of his first client. This was a fifteen year old African-American boy charged with assault. From what Michael could gather, the evidence suggested the boy physically attacked another boy at school. Both students were arrested. Michael wondered why the boy hadn't already been released to his parents. He received his answer when he read that the child was living in foster care. He sighed heavily. Without parents willing to assume responsibility for the child, the chances of him being released were slim to none. When his client's turn came, the judge ruled as Michael expected. The boy could be released into the custody of the foster parents, or the State of North Carolina. Either way the young man was screwed until Michael could figure out who was going to assume responsibility for him.

His second case was similar to the first. A thirteen year old Caucasian boy had been arrested for shoplifting. It wasn't the shoplifting that landed him in adult court as opposed to the juvenile system where youthful offenders belong. No, the issue was the subsequent attack on the arresting officers. When Michael looked at the boy, he didn't look capable of breaking away from an officer and hitting him in the head with a brick. The boy looked small and innocent. As with his first client, this child also lacked loving parents. A fact that made Michael's heart twist in his chest. He felt his hand go to the spot as if his touch could soothe the internal ache.

The third and final case of the day involved a seventeen year old African-American boy charged with possession of a controlled substance with intent to sell or distribute. The boy had the build of a basketball player as he stood nearly seven feet tall. Michael wondered why he would resort to throwing his life away when he could probably play a sport that is often a ticket to a much better life than the boy ever imagined. The answer to that question popped up when Michael read that the boy confessed to selling drugs to help his mom with bills after his father was killed in a car crash. With no previous criminal record and a mother willing to assume responsibility for her son, Michael was able to get his client David Sanders released while he waited for his trial. He didn't know how he was going to do it, but Michael was certain he was going to help David and his family.

Tired and emotionally drained from his cases, Michael walked back to the office with a little less pep in his step. Three cases, all three involved children. Michael knew there were basically parentless children in the world, but he had never interacted with them before. He'd never looked into their faces and examined the hopelessness in their eyes. Despite his differences with his parents, the whole day made him grateful for their influence on his life, however misguided it may be.

Michael pulled out his phone and called his mother. She answered on the first ring.

"Michael darling, I have been trying to reach you for days. Why haven't you returned my calls? I've been worried sick."

Michael chuckled. "My apologies Mother, I've been a little overwhelmed with my new job."

"New job? What on earth are you talking about child?"

"Dad didn't tell you? Ha! I should have known. He fired me."

"Fired you? He can't fire you, you're his son!"

"I am aware of that, but in exchange for him making that little situation vanish, he pulled some strings to get me assigned to community service. I'm working in the public defender's office."

"Public defender? You mean like legal aid for low life criminals?"

Michael chuckled again. The incredulousness in his mother's voice was exactly what he expected. "Actually, I'm working with kids and it's why I called you. I saw my first clients today and they each had one thing in common…parents that were not up front and center in their lives. I realized something today Mom, I didn't make the mistakes they made because of you. I just want to say thank you."

"Oh nonsense son, no one in our family has ever behaved the way those people do. Stop your babbling. You are an Ayers. Our worst generation would never be caught around people like that."

Michael sighed. He knew his mother was arrogant and out of touch with reality, but he didn't expect her to be so cruel hearted towards children she'd never met. He needed to end the call before he said something he'd regret later. "Ok Mother. I need to go now. I have more work to do before I leave for the day."

"Michael aren't you listening to me? Stop what you are doing right now and leave that dreadful place. No son of mine will be working in a filthy public defender's office. I will be speaking to your father at once!"

"Alright Mother. Do what you have to do with Dad, but I really must go now. I just wanted you to know that I love you and I'm grateful for all you've done for me."

"Michael Ayers, I know…."

Michael hated to do so, but he ended the call without allowing his mother to finish her thought. He hated the pompous sound in her voice. He sat back in his seat and leaned his head back as he thought about his own personality. Had he been just as mean and hateful as his mother? Was he still that person deep inside? A few days weren't enough to change the moral fiber of a person were they?

***

Three months later…

"All rise, the Honorable Judge Walter Harbison now presiding."

The courtroom came alive with movement as everyone obeyed the order of the bailiff.

"You may be seated," Judge Harbison stated.

Michael took his seat along with everyone else as the familiar judge began the court proceedings of the morning. For the most part the cases were open and shut with nothing out of the ordinary happening. Michael took the additional time to review his newly assigned client's file. Before working for the Public Defender's office, he'd never appeared in court for a defendant he'd never met. Now it seemed to be a routine. He cursed in his mind as he read through the file. The client was only sixteen and being charged with murdering her father. Michael slammed the file close and clinched his fist in anger. What could make a sixteen year old child want to kill her own father? Thomas knew this case would require extensive prep work. It would be unfair to the child for him to defend her with no notice whatsoever. Angrily he reopened the file and began to read more about his client. Her name was Shamika Carrington. She had no prior run-ins with the law, and confessed to the murder when meeting with police. Michael wasn't sure why the case was even assigned to him if the girl had already confessed. What could he do at this point? Michael became so engrossed in his thoughts of the file that he didn't hear Shamika's name being called. When the prosecutor began to speak, Michael's attention returned to the courtroom. The voice he recognized very well was already painting his client as a cold blooded murderer that posed a great threat to society.

"Does the defendant have representation?" Judge Harbison questioned.

"Yes, Your Honor," Michael said standing and rushing to stand next to his scared underage client. "Michael Ayers here for the defense." Michael answered the judge without once looking over at his opponent. He didn't have the time to acknowledge the shock of his opponent's presence in Charlotte as opposed to Raleigh where Michael believed he lived.

The case before him needed his full undivided attention. He'd avoid their usual game of cat and mouse for the sake of focusing on his client.

"Nice of you to join us Mr. Ayers," the judge replied sarcastically. "We are here to discuss the matter of bail."

"Yes Your Honor, in light of the severity of the charges, the people request that the defendant be remanded without bail," the prosecutor stated.

"Your Honor, my client has no history of violence or any other run-ins with the law for that matter. She's a sixteen year old student that does not pose a threat to anyone. Furthermore, given the fact that she comes from an underprivileged family, she is not a flight risk. We request that she be allowed bail."

"I'm sure her deceased father thinks she's a danger to someone," the prosecutor chimed in.

Michael remained quiet. Usually he'd have a snappy remark, but today his focus was singular; get through the bail hearing so he could read more about this case and interview his client.

"I agree with both of you. Bail is set at $500,000 cash or bond." The judged ruled as he banged his gavel. "Next case."

"But You Honor," Michael objected, "My client can't afford a bond that high. She's a kid for Christ's sake."

"Well, your client should have thought of that before she stabbed a man in cold blood! Next case," Judge Harbison roared.

Michael turned to his client whose eyes were wide with fear. For the first time he looked at the girl. She looked smaller than sixteen even through the baggy orange jumpsuit. Her almond shaped eyes were brown and held a mixture of fear and innocence. Her dark skin was smooth and her long hair was pulled back into a messy ponytail. She looked like she belonged on a cheerleading squad, not on trial for murder.

"I'm going to visit you so we can discuss your case okay?" Michael half told, half questioned the girl.

She nodded her head yes as a single tear rolled down her cheek. Michael's heart twisted inside of his chest. That was a first. He'd spent months at a time with previous clients and felt absolutely nothing. Now within minutes, this girl touched him in a way he'd never felt before. This child deserved a happy life, not a life behind bars where her surroundings would turn her into the criminal the justice system already believed she was.

Michael gathered his briefcase and left the courtroom at warp speed. He needed to get back to the office and start working on Shamika's case. He knew nothing about this girl, yet he believed with all of his heart that she was innocent. As he exited the courtroom and headed towards the elevator he heard the voice that always seemed to get under his skin.

"I see you're slumming these days huh?"

Michael stopped and turned to face the prosecutor Bartholomew Winslow. Bart and Michael had a rich history. They grew up together as their fathers built a successful law practice. As boys they were inseparable, both choosing to follow in their fathers' footsteps and attend law school. They daydreamed of taking over the firm when their fathers retired. They were quite the pair until their second year of law school when Bart's father left his mother for a legal secretary. His mother was crushed and committed suicide. The loss of his mother made Bart hate everything and everyone connected to Ayers, Rogers, & Winslow including Michael. Initially Michael hoped time would heal his childhood friend's wounds and they would reconnect, but he gave up hope years ago. Bart grew more vicious each time they saw each other.

"No, Bart. I never slum, but you should already know that."

"I know that Carrington girl can't afford Ayers, Rogers, & Winslow."

"On that point, I can't disagree," Michael said before turning and walking away.

"You know I'm going to win this right? The girl confessed," Bart yelled as Michael hurried into the elevator.

***

"She's sixteen! I can't defend her without extensive prep time."

"We don't have extensive prep time, so you'll have to defend her without it."

"Thomas…"

Thomas raised an eyebrow at the use of his first name.

"Excuse me, Mr. Willoughby, but I've never handled a case like this before. Wouldn't it be better to put one of the other lawyers on this case? Maybe Kate, she has history with juvenile defendants."

"Mr. Ayers, are you saying you aren't capable of providing adequate counsel for this client?"

"No, that's not what I'm saying. I'm saying adequate isn't enough when the client is sixteen and on trial for murder. This case is outside of my realm of expertise."

Thomas laughed a hearty laugh. He laughed so long Michael's face began to twist "Excuse me. It's rude of me to laugh, but it's been a long time since I've heard bullshit spoken so fluently."

"What did you just say to me?" Michael stood and raised his voice as his anger began to overtake him.

"Sit down," Thomas said still chuckling. "You and I both know why you're here. It isn't because of a love for the clients, it's because you screwed up and Daddy sent you here for me to babysit. So don't act all indignant when I call you on that crap you just tried to feed me."

Michael kicked the chair and stormed out of Thomas' office. Day ninety two in his personal hell hole was not turning out to be much better than day one. He rushed back down to his office and grabbed his things before heading to the jail to visit Shamika. Thomas might not believe he cared, but he did. That little girl needed someone to care about her future, and for reasons unbeknownst to him, Michael was determined to be that person.

***

The smell of the interview room made Michael uncomfortable. No matter how many clients he visited during his community service, he never became accustomed to the smell. Ayers, Rogers, & Winslow clients usually went to the firm's headquarters to be interviewed. The small musty interview room in the Mecklenburg County jail was a far cry from the lifestyle to which he was accustomed. Michael took a seat at the small table. While he waited for his client to be escorted in for their private visit, he perused her file once more. Something he hadn't noticed before caught his attention. He grabbed a pen from his briefcase and scribbled a few notes. Just as he wrote the last word, the door opened and his heart stopped at the sight of his client. She looked even more frightened than when he'd seen her in court. She didn't make eye contact with him, but he could still sense her fear.

As Shamika walked towards him, Michael stood and motioned for her to take the seat in front of him. She obliged but still avoided eye contact. Once the deputy that escorted her into the room was safely on the other side of the door Michael jumped head first into his inquiry.

"Why did you stab your father? Was it an accident? Were you defending yourself?"

Shamika sat in silence with her eyes focused on the floor in front of her.

"Shamika, can you tell me anything?"

She remained mute.

"Ms. Carrington," Michael began attempting a show of respect to pull Shamika out of the state she was in. "I'm Michael Ayers, remember me from court today? I'm your attorney. I'll need you to talk to me if we are going to have any hope of getting you out of here."

A tear rolled down Shamika's face, but she didn't say a word, or raise her eyes to meet Michael's searching pupils.

"Shamika, can you tell me anything at all?" Michael probed in a voice that bordered anger.

Nothing.

"How am I supposed to defend you if you won't talk?

Shamika burst into tears. Loud cries of anguish filled the room as a stunned Michael sat unable to speak. He had no clue as to how he could comfort a teenage girl. Wail after wail Shamika cried out until the bailiff came back into the room. Just as quickly as she was escorted in, she was escorted out and Michael still had no idea how to help her.

***

"I don't know how to help her Kate. She wouldn't speak. She just burst into tears." Michael said as he paced in the tiny space behind his desk.

"So she didn't say anything?"

"Have you been listening to me? No! She didn't say a single word," Michael said a little more loudly than he intended.

Kate arched her eyebrow.

"How am I supposed to help her beat this if she won't talk to me? I mean she barely even looked at me," Michael lamented.

"She's probably scared out of her mind."

"She should be! She's facing murder charges when she should be running around a soccer field or practicing for some cheerleading competition."

Kate smiled.

"Why are you smiling?"

"It's nice to see you care about the client."

"Of course I care. All you people keep giving me are kids. I'd have to be a heartless asshole not to care."

Kate stood to leave the room as Michael plopped down into his chair looking completely worn out and disheveled. "There was a time when you behaved like a heartless asshole. I'm glad to see that guy has left the building." Kate walked into the hallway and nearly bumped into Thomas. He placed a finger to his lips requesting her silence. Kate obliged as they both turned and headed for the elevator.

5

Michael made his way into the building that was becoming like a second home. He still hated the dark and dusty place, but it was getting easier and easier to work there now that he had cases that actually mattered to him.

"Good morning Counselor," Tanya said with a smile that scared Michael shitless.

"Uh…good morning," Michael replied hesitantly. Since their first encounter, Michael made it point to stay as far away from Tanya as possible.

"I have your coffee for you," Tanya said standing and leaving the comfort of her receptionist desk. "Ms.

Young said you like it black with sugar," Tanya continued as she handed Michael the coffee.

"Kate told you how I like my coffee?"

"Yes. Why? Is it hard for you to believe that I actually care how you like your coffee?"

"Quite frankly yes. The last time you even spoke to me you threatened to kick my ass and now you're handing me coffee. Pardon me if I seem confused."

Tanya laughed a little too loudly and hit Michael on the shoulder playfully.

As Michael suspected her playful hit was much harder than any woman he'd ever known. The force knocked him slightly off balance and caused his coffee to slosh over the edge of his cup.

"Oh I'm sorry," Tanya said. "I guess I really don't know my own strength. You go on up to your office. I'll clean up this little mess," Tanya said as she moved about looking for napkins.

Michael's confusion registered on his face as he slid his keycard into the door that led to the offices. He walked down the long dusty hallway to his office trying to shake off the encounter he just had with Tanya. He wasn't sure what she was up to but there was no way in hell he was drinking that coffee she gave him. Something inside of him led him to believe she'd spiked it in some way. He had enough experience with angry women to know not to trust sudden nice behavior. He opened the door to his closet office and his heart felt like it leapt into his throat. His belongings were gone. The office he'd spent the last three months trying to get accustomed to was as blank as the day he moved in.

Michael went into the office and sat the coffee cup on the desk. He removed his jacket which he hung on the back of his chair. Without hesitation he walked towards the elevators. As he rode the elevator to the tenth floor Michael gave himself a pep talk. "You must stay calm and think of Shamika. She needs you. Don't go in there pissing off Willoughby. Just ask him for your belongings and be on your merry way. Watch your tone and leave the sarcasm out of your voice."

As soon as the elevator dinged, the effect of the pep talk vanished. An angry Michael stepped out of the elevator and headed straight for Thomas's office. He ignored Thomas's secretary Darlene as she tried to stop him from barging into Thomas' office.

"He's in a meeting," Darlene yelled. "You can't go in there."

"Like hell I can't," Michael yelled back before bursting into Thomas' office.

"Where the hell are my things?' Michael started in on Thomas as soon as he laid eyes on him.

Thomas' face hardened but his voice was steady as he spoke. "Good morning Michael. I'd like you to meet Nadine McCollum. She's a Social Worker with the Mecklenburg County Department of Social Services. She's here to help you with the Carrington case."

Michael's face flushed as he extended his hand to the woman sitting opposite of Thomas. "My apologies Ma'am. Thank you for being here and being willing to help with this case. Shamika could sure use the help and quite frankly so can I."

Nadine shook his hand with the firm grip she used when meeting new people. "I don't mind helping at all darling. This is what I do."

"Oh really? How so?"

"Well for almost thirty years now I've worked for Social Services in various departments. I've seen my share of sad cases, and no matter how difficult the circumstances, I've helped the clients in any way I could. It breaks my heart to see people suffer, but children just steal my heart away. No child should have to suffer abuse when there are so many barren women in the world praying for their chance at becoming a mother."

"Nadine is being modest," Thomas chimed in. "She has single handedly rescued and nurtured thousands of children in her lifetime."

"Oh stop it Thomas," Nadine said with a smile that displayed a hint of embarrassment.

"Well Ms. McCollum, if there has ever been a child that needs your help, Shamika is that child. She's facing a murder charge."

"What did she say when you met with her?" Thomas inquired.

"Nothing. She wouldn't talk. She just started crying. I couldn't get her to stop."

"Oh dear. What about her parents?" Nadine asked.

"That's the problem," Michael replied. Her mother is nowhere to be found, and her father is the man she's accused of killing."

Thomas cleared his throat. "I don't want to be rude, but I have an appointment I can't miss. Why don't you two move this conversation down the hall. Michael, I'll check in with you later this afternoon for the update."

"To the conference room? Isn't there a meeting in there this morning?"

"No, not the conference room," Thomas said as he stood and grabbed his suit jacket off of the back of his chair. "There is an office you can use three doors down from here. It's on the right."

Michael and Nadine both stood to leave Thomas' office. Michael was still pissed about his office being cleared out, but he needed time to speak with Nadine while she was available. They walked the short distance to the office Thomas directed them to and Michael immediately smiled upon entering. Not only were his things from downstairs in the office, but a number of items from his office at Ayers, Rogers, & Winslow adorned the large beautifully decorated space. The window gave him a view of downtown Charlotte that was absolutely beautiful. Michael wanted to stand and stare out of the window, but he knew he had to focus and get down to business with Nadine. He sat down at the desk he assumed as now his and motioned for Nadine to take a seat across from him. He rummaged through the desk searching for a pen and pad. Upon finding them the questions began pouring out of him.

"So Ms. McCollum, based on your experience how can I get my client to talk to me?"

Nadine laughed. "First, stop calling me Ms. McCollum. No one calls me that. Nadine will do just fine. Second, stop pretending you don't want to take a moment and enjoy this office. Thomas told me he finally moved you out of the broom closet."

Michael twisted his face.

"Oh you thought you were the only one forced to work out of that dust bucket?" Nadine laughed even harder. "Chile Thomas has been hazing people with that thing for years. Just about everyone working here started right down there."

"Why?"

"It's Thomas' way of figuring out who is here for the clients and who is here for a paycheck. I'm sure you don't know this, but fifty years ago when Thomas was just a little boy his father was wrongfully convicted. Back in those days black men had a hard time simply existing in our country but it was even worse when they were accused of a crime. Anyway, Thomas' father was the sole breadwinner for the family so when they arrested him the family barely had money for food, let alone a good attorney. Though he was just a boy, Thomas became hell bent on becoming a public defender. It wasn't enough for him to simply work in this office. He wanted to run things so that he could ensure every defendant, right or wrong, received the representation they deserved."

Michael sat back in his chair and pondered Nadine's words. "And the kids? Why does he start us out defending kids?"

"What better way to soften your heart than to show you a child in need of help?"

For the first time Michael smiled.

"What is that smile about?"

"His plan worked. I've never cared about a client like I care about these kids and I didn't even realize this was Thomas' goal. I just thought he hated me."

"Trust me, if Thomas hated you, you wouldn't be here. Now, let's get down to business. Tell me what you know about your client Shamika Carrington."

***

Michael sat in the waiting room still repulsed by the smell, but grateful he wasn't alone this time. Having Nadine with him gave him confidence. The time he spent with the woman made him feel relaxed, if that was any indication of the affect she'd have on Shamika, they were in the clear. Michael took a moment to look over at Nadine. Her fire red hair was pulled into a tight bun and her deep blue eyes looked sharp and focused. He was sure she could feel him staring at her, but she did not acknowledge him. She stared intently at the door. Many questions regarding Nadine's background swirled in his mind, but he knew better than to ask her. Today was about Shamika.

Michael returned his focus to Shamika's file. Since meeting with Nadine two days ago, they'd gathered quite a bit of information about the girl. For one, they now knew she attended Independence High School, but her performance there was subpar. She didn't have a single friend to be found and most of her teachers described her as a shy introvert. Her English teacher on the other hand pointed out stories that

Shamika wrote. Regardless of the assignment, Shamika wrote stories filled with spelling errors about a teenage female superhero that protected the younger children around her. Michael was clueless about the meaning or relevance of the stories, but Nadine seemed to understand them perfectly.

As the door of the interview room opened, Michael's eyes went wide with terror. He rushed over to Shamika.

"What the hell happened to her?" he yelled at the guard.

"How should I know? She was like this when I went to get her," the cavalier guard responded

"Shamika who did this to you?"

Shamika raised her head slightly but did not speak. Michael's anger soared as he looked at the bruises on her face and her swollen lips.

"You mean to tell me no one knows how her face got like this? I was just here two days ago and she looked fine. I'm her attorney. You know that? Her attorney!

I'll hold every person in this building responsible for the mistreatment of my client until someone suddenly remembers what happened to her!" Michael was breathing heavy and screaming at the top of his lungs.

Shamika began to sob lightly.

"That's enough Michael," Nadine said sternly.

Michael turned to see Nadine standing and staring at the guard with fury in her eyes. "You can leave us now and see that we are not disturbed while we speak with this child."

The guard left without a single word. Something in Nadine's voice demanded respect and obedience. Michael stood frozen in his spot embarrassed and angry with himself for losing his temper in front of Shamika. Nadine left her spot at the table and walked over to Shamika.

"Hello Shamika. My name is Nadine and I'm a social worker. I've helped my share of people in situations like yours over the years. Michael and I have gathered a little bit of information about you, but I'd much rather hear it from you. Would you be willing to speak with me?"

Shamika nodded her head yes. Nadine turned and motioned for Shamika to follow her to the table. Michael remained in place admiring Nadine for how she switched into caregiver mode. One minute her voice was strong and commanding, the next it was soft and encouraging. Michael was amazed the middle aged woman had both weapons inside of her small frame.

Nadine and Shamika both took their seats at the table. Nadine glanced quickly at Michael. She didn't say a word or move an inch, but Michael knew that was his clue to join them. He moved to the table and took his seat next to Nadine. Once he was seated Nadine seemed ready to begin. Content with her ability to even get Shamika to nod, Michael decided to play the role of observer during this meeting. Clearly the skilled social worker would be ten times more effective than he ever could.

"Shamika, is it okay if I ask you a few questions?"

Shamika nodded her head yes.

"Can you tell me your full name?"

Shamika scrunched up her face.

"Please, I know it sounds silly, but can you do that for me?"

"Shamika Diane Carrington," the girl squeaked out while looking down at the floor.

"Okay Shamika Diane Carrington, how old are you?"

"Sixteen."

"Great. And you attend Independence High School, is that correct?"

Shamika nodded her head.

"Sweetie, no one can hear you nod. You have a beautiful voice, please let it be heard," Nadine said gently.

Shamika made eye contact with Nadine for the first time. Michael feared she would respond harshly, but instead she simply said, "Yes, I go to Independence."

"We talked to some of your teachers there. They all said you are pretty quiet. Do you agree?"

Shamika nodded her head. When Nadine didn't reply, Shamika looked into her eyes again. "Yeah," Shamika said.

"Are you quiet at home too?"

"I have to be quiet at home. Daddy doesn't like to hear my voice."

"What about your mom Shamika? Does she live with you?"

"She did, but she left that night."

"That night? Do you mean the night your father was killed? Do you think you can tell us what happened that night?"

Shamika's eyes grew wide with fear.

"It's okay Shamika. You are safe here with Michael and me. We are here to help you."

Shamika stared down at the floor for so long Michael feared she'd never say anything. As soon as he opened his mouth to break his role as observer Shamika began to speak.

"I tried to keep it a secret. I didn't want him to know, but he caught me in that lie and that made him so angry. He started screaming and throwing things. He told me he wasn't going to let some little tramp ruin him. He said it probably was from some boy at school, but I've never been with a boy at school. I knew he would be mad when he found out so I tried to hide it, but I couldn't keep faking the blood so he figured it out."

Nadine's voice was slow and steady. "Shamika, what did Lamar figure out?"

Shamika shook her head. "I can't tell you. Every time I tell someone something bad happens."

"Nothing bad is going to happen to you while Michael and I are here," Nadine said as she reached out and touched Shamika's hand. "Tell us Shamika. What did Lamar figure out?"

Shamika started to cry and shake her head. "You don't understand. I can't. It's all I have."

"What's all you have?" Michael interjected.

Shamika's eyes darted to Michael whose presence she'd ignored for the last few minutes. She stared at him as if she were trying to decide whether or not she could trust him. After a long uncomfortable silence she spoke.

"My baby! My baby is all I have! Daddy said if people knew I was pregnant they would take my baby away because no one lets kids keep babies, but that's not true. Tasia at my school had a baby last year and I saw pictures of the baby in her locker. She talks about the baby all the time so I know they let her keep it. But Daddy said I couldn't keep mine. He was going to stick a clothes hanger inside of me. He said the mess in my stomach had to come out. I didn't want him to kill my baby, so when he came at me I stabbed him with the knife. I didn't want to kill him I just wanted to stop him from killing my baby. It's all I have. No one loves me. My baby will love me. I couldn't let him kill my love!" Shamika's breathing was labored as she continued to cry.

Nadine got up and moved to where Shamika was sitting. She wrapped her arms around the teenager and let Shamika cry into her bosom. Michael sat stunned to silence at the tale Shamika just told. It was farfetched but he believed every word. The girl didn't look pregnant but that was probably due to her still being early in the pregnancy. He pulled out his note pad and began jotting notes. So many questions swam around in his head. He needed answers to help prepare Shamika's defense. Knowing she stabbed Lamar in defense of her child meant he could easily argue she wasn't guilty by reason of self-defense. Hell, in his opinion the D.A. should have never pressed charges. Maybe he could get the charges dropped and Shamika would never have to go to trial. She could be released so that she could have her baby in peace and finish high school. Michael stopped writing and looked up at Nadine. He needed to ask Shamika just two questions. As if she read his mind, Nadine stepped back and gently lifted Shamika's head so that their eyes could connect.

"I know this is difficult sweetheart, but Michael needs to ask you just a few more questions."

Michael didn't bother waiting for Shamika to respond. "Shamika, you said every time you told someone something bad happens. Who else did you tell about your baby?"

"The police," Shamika revealed as she wiped her tears away with the backs of her hands.

Michael exchanged glances with Nadine. "And you said your mom left that night. Did she leave before or after you stabbed Lamar?"

"After. I went downstairs to tell her what happened. When she saw all the blood she started screaming and calling me a murderer. She packed her suitcase, then called the police right before she left."

"She hasn't come to visit you or checked on you at all?"

"No," Shamika said before breaking down again.

"That's enough for today," Nadine said with finality. "Shamika, I promise you I am going to do everything in my power to get you out of here as soon as possible and when I do I'm going to make sure no one ever hurts you like this again. Can you hold on just a little while longer?"

Shamika nodded her head.

Nadine moved to the door and knocked to notify the guard that their meeting was over. Michael had more to say, but he followed Nadine's lead. Once Shamika was safely out of the room Nadine turned to Michael. "Draw up the request for a second bail hearing. We're getting her out of here ASAP!"

"On what grounds?"

"Were you not just listening? The police withheld evidence! They didn't mention the baby or the fact that Lamar threatened to give Shamika an illegal abortion. They painted her to be a cold blooded killer. We're going back before the judge with the truth!"

"I want Shamika out of here just as bad as you do, but there is no guarantee the judge will change his mind. Everything Shamika just told us is unsubstantiated."

"Unsubstantiated or not, my name is respected in this city. I've investigated more child abuse cases than anyone else in the state of North Carolina. I know what I'm doing and I guarantee any judge you allow me to speak to will release that girl into my care. Now set it up!"

6

"It's a little odd seeing you here with the defense Ms. McCollum. You're normally a witness for the State," Judge Harbison said as Michael, Nadine, and Bart sat before him in his chambers.

"That's correct your Honor, but I was contacted by the defense in this case and after conducting my investigation, I believe there are mitigating circumstances that were conveniently left out when young Ms. Carrington was arrested and charged."

"Oh this should be interesting," Bart interrupted.

"Ms. McCollum," Judge Harbison began, "What type of mitigating circumstances?

"Well for starters Shamika was abused for years by her father. Secondly she's now pregnant and according to her she stabbed Lamar Carrington in self-defense after he threatened to perform an abortion on her with a rusty clothes hanger."

"Wait a minute," Bart yelled. "This is all unsubstantiated."

"So, you admit the girl already told the police she was pregnant and they failed to include that information in her file?" Michael was a little too eager to interject.

"I didn't admit anything. I can't speak for the officers that handled Ms. Carrington's arrest but I can assure you that accusing the Charlotte Mecklenburg Police Department of misconduct is completely uncalled for."

Michael sucked his teeth. The last thing he wanted to do was make this personal, but had it not been for the misconduct of a CMPD detective he wouldn't even know who Shamika Carrington was. "We're not here to accuse the CMPD of anything, but there is the matter of the mishandling of evidence. Apparently there is no DNA from Lamar Carrington on file, which is very hard to believe given the fact that he was stabbed to death. Also, we have yet to see the full confession tape. If you're so sure the officers did not do anything wrong, hand over the full video."

"We already have," Bart replied smugly.

"I find that hard to believe given the fact that Shamika was taken from her home for questioning around 10pm. She wasn't actually charged and booked until 8am, yet your so-called full confession video is only thirty minutes long. In that ten hour time span you're telling me the girl was only questioned for thirty minutes?"

"No, I'm telling you her confession was the only thing recorded and it was thirty minutes."

"So CMPD just forgot to turn the camera on until just moments before Shamika confessed," Michael challenged with his usual air of arrogance.

"Your Honor," Bart said turning his attention away from Michael, "I'm not sure what these two have cooked up, but as I'm sure you are aware the Charlotte Mecklenburg Police Department is one of the most respected police forces in the state. An allegation such as this is completely off base."

"Allegation or not, while investigating Shamika's case, I found substantial evidence that indicates the child has been abused. Had this case been handed to me prior to that awful night I would have recommended she be removed from the home. Here is my full report," Nadine said as she leaned forward and handed the judge a large stack of papers.

"Your Honor the State has not been given the opportunity to review that report," Bart said with incredulity.

"Relax Mr. Winslow, this is not being entered into evidence yet. At this point we are only trying to get Shamika's bail reduced so that she can receive proper medical care and tutoring services. The child desperately needs both since there is no record of either being provided for the last ten years of her life. She's not the cold blooded killer you are trying to make her out to be. She is a victim and you should be ashamed of yourself for allowing her to be victimized all over again. Do you know she was attacked while in lock up?" Nadine challenged.

"Inmates fight. Unless you happen to have allegations against the Mecklenburg County Sherriff's Department in that file of yours as well, we can't hold the county responsible for criminals behaving as criminals."

"Enough!" Judge Harbison had enough of the bickering from both sides. "I will take some time to review this file in private. In the meantime, Ms. McCollum I am ordering you to submit a copy of this same file to the prosecutor's office immediately. You will be notified once I have made my decision."

***

One day later…

"Mr. Winslow have you had a chance to review Ms. McCollum's report?"

"Yes your Honor."

"And do you have any objections to it being used for the purposes of this ruling?"

"No your Honor."

"Great. Given the findings of Ms. McCollum's investigation, I am lowering Ms. Carrington's bail from $500,000 to $50,000. This is still a very serious crime, but it appears there is evidence of abuse which may correlate to Shamika's claim of self-defense. Mr. Winslow if I were you, I'd dig a little deeper before this trial begins. Be sure you want to be known as the prosecutor who put a potential victim on trial for murder. As for you Mr. Ayers, another stipulation of Shamika's release is she must be released into the custody of a court appointed guardian. With her mother being M.I.A. we must find someone to assume responsibility for her since she is still a juvenile. Are we clear?"

"Yes your Honor," Michael, Bart, and Nadine all replied in unison.

"Then the matter is settled. You will be notified when the trial date is set. Now if you will excuse me I am due back in court. This meeting is adjourned."

***

"What the hell do you mean there is only $4,000 in my bank account? How is that possible?" Michael yelled at the bank teller. He'd never paid much attention to his finances as money was always there and the family accountant paid all of his monthly expenses. "Where the hell did all of my money go?"

"Sir, if you would, please follow me."

Michael turned to see a well-dressed man who appeared to be the manager standing next to him. Immediately behind the manager stood a security guard. Michael looked around to see all eyes were fixed on him. Embarrassment crept up his cheeks as reality settled within him. He dropped his head as he followed the manager into his office.

Once they were safely tucked away in the manager's office Michael began yelling again.

"Do you know who I am? My family's money has built branches of this bank. My grandfather was one of the first major investors. How dare you treat me like a common criminal summoning your piss poor security like I am about to rob the place!"

"Sir, I can assure you that was not our intent at all. I simply wanted to pull you to the side so that we can discuss your financial matters in the privacy of my office. As you mentioned, I am well aware of your family's interests here in this bank. I would never assume you would ever want or need to steal anything."

Michael wasn't buying the bullshit the portly bank manager was selling, but he remained silent as the man typed into his computer. After what appeared to be a long while the manager began to speak again.

"I think I see what the problem is."

"Okay, well don't hold it in, spill it. Where the hell is my money?"

"It appears your personal checking account is receiving significantly less in monthly contributions."

"What!"

"Yes sir. For several years now, you received two monthly deposits. One in the amount of $15,000 that was automatically transferred from your trust account, and a second Ayers, Rogers, & Winslow payroll deposit of $8,500. But about three months ago both deposits stopped. Since then there have been counter deposits of $5,000 cash on the first of the month."

Michael stood and left the bank without another word. Fueled by fury he headed straight to the responsible party. It was one thing for his father to fire him, it was another for him to embarrass him by taking away money that was rightfully his. Bruce Ayers was finally about to see the wrath of his only child and based on the rage coursing through Michael's veins, it wasn't going to be pretty.

***

"You had no right stopping my Trust deposits. That money was left to me by Grandfather. It has nothing to do with you, you controlling hypocrite."

"Hypocrite? You dare waltz your spoiled entitled ass into my office and insult me? Me! Your own father! If it weren't for me, you'd still be the same whining snot nosed kid that held on to your nanny's apron strings. How dare you speak to me this way!" Bruce Ayers roared so loud at Michael his voice could be heard all over the office.

"No, if it weren't for you and your urge to teach me a lesson I wouldn't have just had to pick my face up off of the floor at the bank!" Michael flared his arms about as he imitated his father as he spoke.

"You listen here you little shit," Bruce Ayers said as he rose from his seat. "You will remember that I am your father and you will watch the way you speak to me or the $5,000 deposits will stop. You think you'll manage with no money you spoiled entitled ingrate! I don't owe you anything! Everything I live off of I built with my own blood, sweat, and tears. Do you even know what it feels like to become a success? No! You don't! And you want to know why? Because your mother and grandfather laid the fucking red carpet out for you since birth. You're a boy playing a man's game, lying and bending the rules as it suits you. Well I finally had enough. I'm sick of your silver spoon shit! I'm going to make a man out of you if I have to do it from my death bed. Now get out of my office before I have security throw you out."

Michael's eyes glossed over. The tears rose but he refused to let them fall. He took a step towards the door before turning to his father one final time. "My whole life I aspired to be you. I became an attorney because of you, daydreamed of becoming partner in your firm! I did everything I could to get you to see that I am a damn good attorney. I pushed the limits to make you believe in me, but you never did. You think you're done? No, I'm the one that's done! Do what you want with your money. I'll never ask you for anything else, not even your love you self-righteous son of a bitch."

Michael stormed out of his father's office and avoided eye contact with the nosey staff. The last thing he wanted was to answer the questions he saw in their eyes. He went to his old office and gathered the last of his belongings. Any hope he held out regarding returning to the firm officially vanished as he stood in his father's office moments earlier. The boxes that sat on the floor next to his old desk told him his father gave up hopes long before he did.

As he packed the last box he heard a commotion outside of the office. He stopped packing for a moment and paused to listen. He thought of going to see what the issue was, but he quickly changed his mind and returned to packing. The sooner he left the building the better. He needed distance between himself and his father.

"Michael, it's your dad! He collapsed," a young person Michael had never seen before yelled from his now open doorway.

Michael stopped packing and started rushing towards the door. As he caught a glimpse of himself in the mirror he stopped. He wandered closer to the mirror his mother purchased for his office his first day at the firm and examined his reflection. When did those lines creep up around the corner of my eyes? He thought to himself. When did I start to resemble my father so much? He took his hand and rubbed the lines as if they were a figment of his imagination. Nope he felt them as well, so they must be real. He stared into his eyes and wondered when they became so serious. He caught the furrow in his brow and tried to relax a little, but it remained.

"Michael, come on. The paramedics are on the way, but he's asking for you," the young man at the door insisted.

"I'm not going," Michael replied still looking into the mirror.

"What?"

"I'm not going. My father made it clear that he wanted me to leave, so I'm honoring his wishes." Michael smiled as the words left his lips. He straightened his tie before leaving the mirror. He went back to his old desk and picked up a picture of his mother before turning to leave.

"Tell the old man they can throw the rest out, I have all I need from this place," He said as he headed for the elevator with a smile.

***

"Nadine you did what?!"

"I paid the child's bail. She's here with me."

"Nadine, I don't mean to sound rude…"

"Then don't," the fiery woman said cutting Michael off mid-sentence.

Michael took the phone away from his ear as he inhaled deeply. He didn't want to upset his newly found ally, but he couldn't risk Shamika going back to jail because of something Nadine did. He gathered his thoughts before returning the phone to his ear and continuing. "I'm just trying to make sure we have followed the Judge's every order. Shamika is supposed to be released to a court appointed guardian. How could you find someone this quickly, and have time to have a court hearing?"

"Michael I'm surprised you haven't done your homework on me by now. I am one of the strongest pillars of this community when it comes to the safety and welfare of children. I've dedicated my life to ensuring the children of this city do not suffer one moment longer than necessary. I have a strong network and an even stronger reputation. Did you not take notice of Judge Harbison's reaction to me?"

Michael rubbed his temple with his free hand. "All of that is wonderful Nadine, but what is Shamika doing with you? Why isn't she with this guardian you supposedly found?" He didn't intend for the sarcasm to slip out, it just did. The day had been taxing and listening to Nadine speak in riddles was the last thing he felt like doing.

"If you're so ignorant that you can't figure that out, I may need to speak to Thomas about assigning this child a new lawyer. Now go work on this girl's case and stop asking me stupid questions!" Nadine ended the call abruptly.

More confused than when he initially called, Michael attempted to take solace in the fact that Shamika was out of jail. The county lock up was no place for a pregnant sixteen year old. Now that he knew her immediate safety had been secured, Michael made the call he didn't want to make.

"Hello Michael. I'm happy you called. How are you son?"

"Hello Mother. I would like to say that I am well, however Father has made that a bit difficult for me to say without lying."

"Oh really?"

"Yes Mother. I'll cut to the chase. Father cut off my access to my Trust Fund. At my age, I no longer need a Trust Fund in the first place. The money should have been released to me ages ago, but because of my earnings from the firm I never bothered to question his decision to ration out my inheritance. Now since he's decided to teach me a lesson I was thoroughly embarrassed at the bank today when I learned I don't even have enough money in my checking account to cover my basic expenses. How does he expect me to live?"

"I'm appalled your father would go to such lengths, but I really shouldn't be. He's been acting rather strange of late. I'll call the accountant and have funds wired into your account immediately. In the meantime, if you want access to your Trust Fund again, you'll need to do as I've instructed."

"What instruction mother?"

"Leave that Godforsaken place your father has you working at and go back to Ayers, Rogers, & Winslow. You don't belong at some legal aid office with criminals and scoundrels. You're an Ayers, more importantly you have my father's blood in your veins and Henry Hawthorne never lowered his standards for anyone…"

Michael's thoughts drifted away as his mother continued her rant. His whole life he'd listened to her go on and on about her family's influence and rich blood line. He could name his ancestors all the way back to the days of slavery and all of their stories were the same. Rich man married woman from an equally rich family and they continued to live in wealth until they both died. At which time they passed the wealth on to their children who walked in their footsteps. Growing up, his family's history brought him joy. Now, in the wake of his newly found social awareness he felt utterly embarrassed. How could families that were given so much ignore those that were given so little? More importantly, how had he lived completely unaware of the social issues in his own city for so long?

On the surface he knew there were poor people in the world. He knew all about the welfare system and how his tax dollars supported people who couldn't or wouldn't provide for themselves. He knew about the higher crime rates in poor neighborhoods. He rarely read the newspaper, but he'd heard about children committing serious crimes before. What he never thought of was the correlation between the less fortune of the parents and the behaviors of the children living in substandard conditions. Children raised in poverty and crime stricken neighborhoods grow up believing their way of life is the only way of life, just as he'd grown up believing his way was the only way. Michael scratched his head. How could he have remained so aloof his whole life?

"Michael, are you listening to me?" Margaret Ayers' voice jolted Michael back into the moment.

"Yes Mother. I am listening, but I don't think you're going to like my response."

"Nonsense. Come have dinner with me this evening and we can discuss this further."

A new thought came to Michael. "Mother, are you not going to the hospital?"

"Hospital? Heaven's no. Why would you ask me such a question?"

Michael opened his mouth to speak, but snapped it shut just as quickly. He remained silent for a moment while staring into the distance. His mind raced until he finally gave up his quest for understanding. With slumped shoulders he reluctantly agreed to dinner with his mother. As soon as the words left his mouth he regretted them.

7

Michael sat at his parent's dinner table feeling like a fish out of water. The last time he visited his parent's home was the night of his arrest. That night his father chose to believe the worst about him. No matter how hard he tried to push the thoughts of disappointment out of his mind, his father's disapproving glare was permanently etched into his memory.

Michael glanced around the dining room in which he'd consumed more meals than he'd ever be able to count. The expensive paintings and furnishing that adorned the room seemed to have lost their ability to impress him. The room easily held more than one hundred thousand dollars of valuables, but not a single ounce of love and commitment to the betterment of mankind could be found. Michael sighed as he waited for his parents to join him. He wanted nothing more than for the night to quickly end so he could put the entire house and all of its memories behind him.

"You know your mother would have a cow if she heard you sighing that way at her dinner table."

Michael turned to see Voncelle, the Ayers family maid standing in the doorway. He stood and rushed to her side.

"Voncelle, I haven't seen you in ages," he exclaimed as he wrapped his arms around the petite woman. "You look exactly the same."

"And I see that tongue of yours is still telling lies," Voncelle replied with a warm smile.

"No, I'm serious. You haven't aged a bit." Michael did in fact notice a few wrinkles at the corners of her dark brown eyes and her once jet black hair now held more grey than he remembered, but her smile still shined as bright as it did when he was a child. "Where have you been? The last few times I stopped by you weren't here. I figured you'd quit."

"Quit? Oh heavens no. Who would take care of your parents if I left? I only work a few days a month now that I'm getting up in my years, but I still make sure things are running smoothly around here. With you out of the picture, there's way less mess for me to clean up," Voncelle added with a chuckle.

Michael's smile faded. "Look, I'm really sorry about all the stuff I put you through." His eyes shifted to the floor the same as they did when he was a child being scolded for one of his many mischievous actions.

Voncelle's mind flashed back to the first time she'd seen that look. Michael was about four years old and had eaten his way through most of the desserts she'd prepared for Sunday dinner. When cornered all he could do was hold his head down in shame and let his tears puddle onto the floor. Though the tears disappeared as he grew older, his expression of shame remained the same. She reached out and grabbed his hand in hers.

"Michael you stole my heart the first time your fat little fingers smeared milk all over my face. You're the closest thing I ever had to a child of my own, and children are expected to lose their way from time to time. What's important is that you find your way back. That look on your face tells me I have my little Mikey back."

Michael looked into her eyes and smiled. He still couldn't understand how his parents' home seemed to always turn him into a child, but the warmth of Voncelle's presence made the evening seem much easier to sit through.

"What are you two over there whispering about?" Margaret Ayers questioned as she entered the room.

"Nothing Mother," Michael responded. "I was just telling Voncelle how good it is to see her again and how sorry I am for behaving so terribly as a teenager," Michael continued as he released the maid's hand and returned to his seat at the table.

"Nonsense! You were an excellent child. You made excellent grades and never once used drugs. You've never brought shame or scandal to our name which is much more than I can say for many of our friends' children." Margaret's voice maintained its usual air of superiority.

Michael ignored her remark. "Can we eat now? I have an early day ahead of me."

"As much as I loathe your father's presence, he is still the head of this family and we will wait for him. Voncelle dear, can you go ahead and bring the food in. Mr. Ayers should be down any minute."

"Yes Ma'am," Voncelle replied before exiting the room.

"Michael darling," Margaret began turning her attention to her son. "As I promised on the phone, I had the accountant wire funds into your account, but that will be the last of the financial backing you'll receive until you return to the firm."

"My father made it clear he does not want me there mother. I can't work there as long as he feels I still need to learn some sort of lesson."

"Your father doesn't have a choice. He's sick. The doctors haven't given him much longer to live, so he'll have to hire you back so that you can run the firm after he's gone."

"I'm not dead yet you insensitive windbag. I'm still alive and I still say he's not worthy of the firm I built from nothing!"

Neither Margaret nor Michael heard Bruce approaching, but his loud voice made his presence evident.

"Don't worry Dad. I have no intentions of ever stepping foot in that place again."

"Great, then it's settled. The boy stays down at the public defender's office until he can prove he's ready to practice law the ethical way," Bruce said as he occupied his seat at the head of the table.

"You can't seriously believe I'm going to allow this foolishness to continue," Margaret replied through clinched lips.

"Mother, it's perfectly okay. What your dear old husband fails to understand is that his firing me was the best thing that ever happened to me. For the first time in my life I care about someone other than myself. All these years I've practiced law and not one single time did I care about the innocence or guilt of my client until now. See, Father here thought he was punishing me, for a crime I did not commit by the way, but what he actually did was free me from the egotistical bullshit he brainwashed into me over the years! You wanna talk ethics old man," Michael questioned as he glared at his father. "Let's talk about all the money you accepted over the years from criminals knowing they were guilty. Let's talk about all of the young secretaries you and your partners have banged right there in the office. Or better yet, let's talk about the extra hours you've billed to every single account, charging clients for hours you spent on the golf course. Is any of that ethical?" Michael stood screaming his accusations at his father who surprised him by remaining seated.

"You're right Michael. It seems I should have fired you years ago. Maybe you would have started your journey to manhood sooner."

"I am a man, you hypocritical bastard!" Michael yelled as he stormed out of the dining room bumping into Voncelle and knocking the plates of food to the floor. He wanted to stop and help her clean the mess, but his anger pushed him forward. He heard his mother call after him, but he didn't bother responding. He hopped into his car and drove to the only place he knew that would help him calm down.

The office was quiet, a welcomed change from the usual hustle and bustle Michael worked through every day. He flipped the light switch in his office and removed his suit jacket, throwing it across the back of a chair. He walked over to the credenza and grabbed the first file box he saw. He needed to work to clear his mind of the mess of a dinner his mother tried to put together. Looking through the box, he retrieved the files he needed and walked over to an empty space by the window. Working on the floor in front of the window always seemed to help him concentrate, so he removed his shoes and plopped down on the floor. He combed through the documents looking for something, anything to help him with Shamika's case. He studied the documents so intently he didn't hear her enter.

"What are you doing here this late?"

Michael jumped at the sound of Kate's voice. She laughed at the startled look on his face. Michael rolled his eyes in irritation.

"I'm working. What does it look like I'm doing?"

"Who pissed in your corn flakes?" Kate asked.

"Look, I came here to work, not be hounded by my underachieving co-workers."

"Well, excuse me for breathing the same air as the latest and greatest Ayers family asshole," Kate said as she turned to leave the office.

"Kate! Wait, I'm sorry. I didn't mean to snap at you. It's just I've had a shitty night so I came here to try to work to take my mind off of things."

"Lady trouble," she half asked, half suggested with a smirk.

"Hell no. The last thing I need right now is a woman. That's what got me here in the first place, a stupid blonde with a big round ass," he huffed as he angrily shuffled through the papers in front of him.

"I don't even know what that is supposed to mean. Look, I'm heading out for some food. Want me to grab you something?"

The mention of food reminded him of his empty stomach. "Yeah, I could eat something," he responded in a much more relaxed tone. "But is it safe for you to go out alone at night?"

"There's a Chinese restaurant right around the corner that stays open late. I grab dinner from there all the time."

"That doesn't mean it's safe. How about you call the order in and I'll walk with you to pick it up."

"If you insist, but remember the last time one of us needed saving I was the one that saved you."

"I was slightly inebriated."

"Sure you were lover boy. What do you want to eat?"

"It doesn't matter as long as it's chicken."

"I have a menu in my office, I'll go call the order in," she said as she walked out the door and back down the hall towards her office.

"And make no mistake," he yelled after her. "I could have hurt her if I wanted to, but I'm a gentleman. I was raised never to hit a lady," he said with a smile before returning to the files spread out on the floor in front of him.

Michael tried to focus on the work in front of him, but it was no use. Kate totally knocked him out of work mode. She always had the ability to steal all of his focus. From the day he met her she captured his attention. He could still remember that day back in college as though it was yesterday. He and Bart had just returned from a Tarheels basketball game. They'd lost to Duke for the third straight game. The whole campus was sullen because of the loss to their most hated rival. They'd gathered outside of his building sitting on the steps and drinking a few beers. Michael was trying his best to shake the loss. It wasn't about the game per se, it was more so the $5,000 he'd bet in favor of his school. He should have known better. As much as he hated to admit it, Duke was having one hell of a season.

Just as he put his bottle to his lips and took the final swig, she walked by. Kate was an instant balm to his wounded ego. As she bounced by him in her tiny tennis skirt laughing with the girl walking next to her he remained frozen and unable to speak. He thought of a great pick up line to yell out to her, but his words were lodged in his throat. He opened his mouth but no sound came out. It was Bart who actually saved him.

"Hello there ladies," Bart started as he jogged up behind them. "I'm Bart. I'm a law student here. My friends and I are drinking away the beating the basketball team just took. Care to join us for a couple cold ones?"

"No," Kate replied with a straight face.

Bart was taken aback. Normally women were putty in his hands. His golden hair, baby blues, and silky voice always seemed to make the ladies go weak in the knees. Sensing his friend was about to strike out for the first time, Michael sprang into action.

"Excuse me ladies what my friend here was trying to say is that before you two walked by we were barely able to string two words together, but the sight of you and the sound of your laughter instantly lifted our spirits. We'd love it if you could share some of that laughter and cheer up a bunch of stressed out law students," Michael said as he flashed his smile directly at Kate. The friend was cute, but Kate was breathtaking. He never took his eyes off of her as she giggled and turned to walk away.

When she was a few feet away from him she turned and yelled over her shoulder, "I'm a law student too. I have to study, no time for hanging with good looking buff guys."

"So you think I'm good looking and buff," Michael yelled after her with a goofy smiled plastered on his face.

Snapping back from the fond memory Michael realized he was wearing the same goofy smile and straightened his face instantly.

"Too late, I saw that smile," Kate interrupted. "What were you thinking about?"

"How great you looked in your tennis skirt the first time I saw you," Michael said with a wink.

She rolled her eyes. "I'm sure you've seen plenty of girls in tennis skirts over the years."

"Yep," he said standing to his feet and walking towards her, "but none of them hold a candle to you." He reached forward and placed one hand on her hip and used the other to tuck a lose strand of hair behind her ear. Kate gasped at his touch. He smiled slightly, thrilled that his touch still affected her.

He leaned in to kiss her, but she backed away quickly. He looked at her with his forehead wrinkled with questions.

"I...I told you... I'm seeing someone," she said as she turned to walk out of his office. "I need to go grab the food. Are you still coming?"

Still unsure about the moment they just shared, Michael grabbed his jacket off of the chair and followed her into the elevator. Neither of them said a word as they made their way downstairs and into the night's chill. Downtown Charlotte was absolutely beautiful at night, but neither of them noticed as they walked in silence. Once they received the food, they started the short trek back to the office.

"What does seeing someone mean?"

"What does it sound like?"

"It sounds like whoever this guy is can't be all that important because we've been working together for months now and I haven't seen him stop by the office or heard you on the phone with him. Hell I haven't even seen a picture of him."

"I told you I take my work seriously. It's all about the clients for me. My boyfriend can wait until I leave the office."

"So now he's a boyfriend?"

Kate rolled her eyes but declined to comment. They walked the remainder of the way in silence.

Back inside of Michael's office they both settled on the floor in front of his file. Neither spoke as they consumed the Chinese food and read over the paperwork in front of them. Kate was the first to break the silence.

"Shamika is pregnant?"

"Yeah," Michael said grimly.

"And she says Lamar was the father… that poor child must be scared out of her mind. How could a father rape his own daughter?"

"That sick fuck was probably an inbreed himself. He was going to rip the baby out with a clothes hanger! A fucking clothes hanger! That's why she stabbed him. His own daughter...he was going to rip her insides to shreds to cover his own ass. What kind of father does something like that to his own flesh and blood?" Michael's faced turned red as he spoke. His hand balled into fists as he stood and paced in front of the window. "It's assholes like that I wish I could get my hands on. It's a good thing Shamika killed him because I would have done it for her by now if he was still alive and that son of a bitch would have died a slow and painful death. "

Kate sat on the floor and watched a side of Michael she'd never seen before. His eyes were cold and dark, his movements purposeful and deliberate. For ten minutes straight Michael stalked about releasing every thought he'd had since learning about Shamika's case. The anger that had been bubbling below the surface was playing out before her like a bad movie.

Kate stood and contemplated leaving but she knew Michael needed her. Caution whispered for her to run in the opposite direction, that she couldn't allow herself to be what he needed, but something else told her to stay, hold him, and soothe his anger with her kisses. She listened to the latter. She took her time walking towards him afraid of what her touch might do to him. He seemed to be in some sort of trance completely unaware that she was still in the room. This was her chance to get out of his way before he began to actually act on his anger. Instead she reached out and grabbed his arm. He stopped moving, but kept ranting without even glancing in her direction. With his eyes fixed on the window, Kate stepped so close that her front was practically melted against his back. Both of her hands closed in around him and traveled to his chest. She could feel his heart beating wildly beneath her touch.

Michael stopped speaking, but his body remained tense and hot beneath her touch. She could literally feel the anger radiating off of him. For a long time they just stood there, him angry and tense, her trying to will him to relax. Finally she lay her head on his back and began to sing. Not a song either of them had ever heard, but the words that flowed from her heart.

"I know what you feel all too well," she sang as she began to stroke his chest slowly and deliberately. "You want to heal the world of all pain. You know the task is too great, so you'll settle for one child…" Kate sang the words of her heart until she had nothing left to offer. She wasn't sure when he relaxed or when the moment became about both of them, but somewhere in her calming him she shared the pain and anguish of her own heart. Michael leaned his head back to rest it on the top of Kate's. Neither spoke as they drunk in the moment. Working on cases that involved children was not for everyone. Any person with a heart would be affected by the things they saw every day. The lengths that some children are forced to go just to survive, is beyond what any person should have to endure. Kate understood the pain that comes from looking into the eyes of a child that is forced into crime to survive, or to weep for the child that gang bangs because no one ever told them they had options. For Kate, the job was more than just a job, and she could now see that whether Michael knew it or not, it was more than just a job for him as well.

"How do you handle it Kate?" He asked in a voice barely above a whisper. She'd never heard him sound so vulnerable. "How do you keep handling these cases year after year? I've only been here a few months and I feel like I'm falling apart at the seams."

"I do what I just did for you. When it gets to be too much, I sing, I write, I run, I play tennis…I do any and everything to clear my heart and mind. Then I focus on how I can help the client. That's what I mean when I say it's all about the clients with me. They need us Michael. Shamika is only the tip of the iceberg."

"I can't think about that, or I'll lose what little bit of my sanity I have left. I've never been a violent man, but I'm pretty sure I'd kill a pedophile or two if I ran into them right now."

"Well I need to make sure we don't let any clients with that charge come near you," Kate said with a giggle.

The sound of her laughter drove Michael over the edge. He turned and covered her mouth with his own before he could stop himself. With ten years of passion, regret, and longing Michael kissed her as if both of their lives were entangled in the kiss. He poured every emotion from his core into her lips. She responded with the same vigor and passion. She wanted to stop herself but her guard was completely down. Her hands traveled to the back of his neck, his to the sides of her face. They stood there caressing and kissing each other until they heard the sound of his voice.

"I guess I shouldn't be surprised to find you two together."

Kate jumped at the sound of his voice and untangled herself from Michael. "Wait…" she attempted to explain, but could not find any other words to say.

He threw back his head and let out what was supposed to be a laugh. "Don't tell me you are going to continue trying to convince me nothing is going on between you two when I just walked in on you."

"It was a kiss Bart. Nothing more. We both got caught up dealing with the emotions of this case and it just happened. It hasn't happened before and it won't happen again."

"The emotions of the case? I hope you're not referring to the case of that sixteen year old murderer. Talking about murder gets you going? If I would have known that I would have done it months ago. At least I would have gotten laid out of the deal. In a few months lover boy over here gets you all hot and bothered at work and after a year of dating all I've gotten is a pair of blue..."

"How dare you!" Kate screamed cutting him off. Her face was red with fury as she slapped Bart's face on her way out of the office.

Michael stood staring at Bart still stunned at all his ears just heard. Kate and Bart dating was too much for him to process with words. He stood waiting for Bart to leave his office. After all he just experienced with Kate, he didn't want to taint the moment trading barbs with the man he once considered his only friend. In true Bart fashion, he wouldn't give Michael the satisfaction.

"I'm not surprised you went after her again," Bart began. "I am a little shocked it took you this long though. The Michael I knew would have had her on her back in ten minutes."

Michael's face twitched in anger, but he remained quiet.

"I struck a nerve? Why have you always pined after her? Let me tell you, she's the same bore you knew in college. Now I see why you banged that red head. Kate is wound so tight, I doubt she's ever let anyone dust her off."

Is he seriously standing here talking to me like we're friends? Michael thought to himself. Then a small smile crept onto his face as he began gathering his belongings. Bart stood wearing a confused expression waiting for him to explain the smile, but Michael would never give him the satisfaction. Happy with Bart's little revelation Michael was heading home to sleep like a baby. Bart's interruption was the perfect cure for the foul mood dinner with his parents put him in. He didn't bother saying goodbye to his intruder, he simply stepped around him and turned the light off on his way out. As he stepped into the elevator he heard Bart yell after him.

"I don't know what that smile was about but you won't be smiling when you read the motion I'm drafting."

Bart kept talking but Michael could no longer hear him after the elevator doors closed. He didn't want to worry but fear crept slowly into his belly. Bart making a motion meant trouble for Shamika's case. They'd just gotten her released, the last thing she needed was Bart troubling the waters.

8

"Nadine, I don't know how you did it, but she looks so much better."

"I gave Shamika what every child wants...love."

"What did the doctor say about the pregnancy?"

"The baby is healthy, but measuring a little small. She's about five months along based on all of their calculations, but the baby seems to be a few weeks smaller. Doc said that could be due to all of the abuse and stress. They're going to keep a close eye on her."

"We need to get a DNA test run before the trial begins. We need evidence that supports Shamika's story," Michael said in a soft rushed tone.

Nadine lowered her voice. "A DNA test while she is still pregnant is risky right? Can't it cause a miscarriage?"

"Nadine, don't hate me for what I am about to say, but would it be the worst thing if this baby did not make it? Shamika is just a kid. A kid who doesn't have a mother. How is she going to be one? How is she going to take care of a baby? She has no education and no skills. And with all of that aside, if we don't get proof that she killed Lamar in self-defense she may go to prison for the rest of her life! Who is going to look after her baby then?"

"Stop talking all of that nonsense! Shamika is not going to prison because you are going to do your job and win this case. As far as the DNA test is concerned, Shamika has rights. If she wants the test now, she can have it. If not, we wait until after the baby is born."

"But…"

"No buts Michael," Nadine said cutting him off. "Shamika has had people abusing and taking advantage of her for as long as she can remember. I'll protect that child and her rights for as long as the good Lord will allow. Shamika," she yelled. "Come in here please."

Michael sat at the small table in Nadine's kitchen stunned into silence. He'd never met anyone quite like Nadine. She was a small framed woman with pale skin and fiery red hair. She seemed to care about children the way that Kate did, if not more. Michael thought for a moment about the way he felt about children. They were not all that important to him before his "incident". That's how he referred to that night in his mind, just an "incident". The incident seemed to be changing his view of people, children included.

Shamika bounced into the room and Michael could have sworn she gained ten pounds seemingly overnight. Her belly still didn't really protrude, but now that she was wearing clothes that actually fit her petite frame, Michael could just barely make out the outline of her small round middle. The dark circles that once decorated her eyes were now gone and there was a hint of something there…hope perhaps.

Her dark hair was once again pulled back into a ponytail, but it now looked well managed and neat. She plopped down into the chair opposite Michael and smiled. It was probably the first genuine smile he'd seen on her face and his heart twisted at the idea of what he wanted to say to her. Whatever Nadine did or said was definitely working. He didn't want to undo any of it. He never wanted to see her cry again, but he had to ask…her life depended on it.

"Hi Shamika," he began shakily. "You look very happy today."

"I am! Did Aunt Nadine tell you? I went to the doctor and she said my baby is healthy. It's a boy! I'm having a little boy. I've already started picking names for him and I have pictures. They gave me pictures of the ultrasound. Wanna see? I'm gonna go grab them for you."

Without waiting for a response, Shamika raced out of the room and down the hall. Michael sighed when she left. There was no way he could say what he originally intended to say. Nadine was right. Shamika had been hurt enough, she deserved this happiness while it lasted.

"What did you give her? She's bouncing off the walls. I couldn't even get a word in."

"This is what a normal happy teenage girl looks like," Nadine said with pride. If Michael didn't know any better he'd think Shamika was Nadine's own flesh and blood. Relation couldn't make a woman more proud than she was at that moment.

***

3 weeks later…

"Your Honor, I don't know how the prosecution knew about this motion, but I can assure you, Mr. Winslow's request to expedite this trial is only a ploy to prevent us from being able to run the DNA test," Michael pleaded with Judge Harbison.

Michael and Bart had both been summoned to the Judge's chambers. As he sat in front of the judge's massive oak desk Michael's palms became sweaty. He was never one for nerves, but this case meant more to him than anything he'd experienced in his 34 years of life.

"Counselor, I'm inclined to agree with the defense on this. In the interest of getting it right here, wouldn't it be in the State's best interest to investigate the girl's claim of self-defense?"

"With all due respect Your Honor, the CMPD conducted a thorough investigation, and there is no evidence to support the claim of self-defense. Even if the DNA confirms the baby belongs to the father, Shamika had choices other than killing her father. The girl had a knife hidden under her mattress as if she was waiting for him. She could have run or told someone at school. She chose to kill him. That is premeditation Your Honor."

"She was a scared kid, not a cold blooded killer! The man abused her for years and no one, NO ONE came to her defense. She felt alone and helpless! Hell, her own mother disappeared after she stabbed him. No one has seen or heard from her. If her own parents abused and neglected her, how was she supposed to know other adults wouldn't do the same? Shamika has no history of violence, no signs of psychotic issues. She was and still is a scared teenage girl that wants to protect her unborn child. Even though the child is a product of rape, Shamika loves the baby and wants to protect it. She's more of a parent at sixteen than her parents ever were to her."

"The alleged rape," Bart interjected.

"If we exhume the body we can run a DNA test to prove Lamar is the father of the baby."

"Enough!" Judge Harbison roared. "My chambers is not the place for you two to argue your case. Mr. Winslow, I have to agree with the defense on this. This is a sixteen year old girl here. Before we move forward with charging this young person with first degree murder as you are alluding to here today, we need to make sure this is handled properly. The last thing we need is a public outcry for mistreatment of a child. I've sat on the bench for thirty years. This is my last go round. I won't have my legacy muddled by the fumbling of this case. Your motion is denied. Mr.

Ayers, your motion to exhume the body for DNA testing is granted. I want the DNA test run as soon as possible."

"Your Honor," Bart chimed in. "I urge you to reconsider…"

Judge Harbison held up his hand with his palm facing Bart, effectively ending the conversation. "I have to get into the courtroom. This meeting is adjourned."

Michael and Bart filed into the hallway outside of the judge's chambers.

"You son of a bitch! You'd ruin the life of a child just because you caught me kissing Kate. I knew you were an asshole, but I never thought you'd sink so low."

Bart sneered. "You think that tease is worth all of this? If she wants to take her chances with scum like you, that's her business. No Michael, this is about justice. You, your father, my father…lawyers like you give the good guys like me a bad name. You go around screwing anything with a pulse. You bend the rules and flush ethics down the toilet. You throw money at every case and keep your criminal clients out of prison where they belong. Well, you won't twist this case. Shamika Carrington is a murderer that killed her own father without batting an eye. Have you even viewed the confession tape?"

"If you're referring to the piss poor video where CMPD coaxed Shamika into giving her account of the night, yeah. I watched it. What's your point?" Michael shifted his weight restless with Bart's conversation.

"Then you already know what I'm talking about. Only sociopaths discuss the cold blooded murder of their father without so much as a single bead of sweat. Your client didn't even appear fazed. You may have the judge fooled, but once I play that confession tape for the jury, she's as good as convicted!"

Bart turned and walked away with a smile on his face. All of Michael's optimism for the case was gone. Not only did he have to deal with Bart, but he had to convince Shamika to do the DNA test as soon as

Lamar's DNA was extracted. Based on his last conversation with her, that was not going to happen.

***

Michael sat in his car which was parked in Nadine's driveway. He held his phone in his hand and stared at the screen pretending to be reading emails. Instead he was searching for the strength to convince Shamika to do the DNA test. She needed the test. She needed the results to prove Lamar was the father of her child. With Bart now on the case like a shark circling new blood, the girl would need tangible evidence of the abuse. As it stood, there were no police or medical records to prove anything other than neglect which wasn't grounds to murder a parent. He shuddered hard at the thought of a daughter living in fear of her own father. He had no children or plans to become a father anytime soon, yet every time he thought of Shamika and the abuse she suffered a protective anger rose up inside of him. He'd never felt this feeling, never cared about the welfare of anyone else, never thought himself capable of caring for a child, but his interaction with Shamika changed that. Her pain was changing him, and in a good way.

Just as he gathered enough courage to go into the house with his speech thought out and well-rehearsed, his phone rang. He looked down at the screen and saw his mother's face and name. He didn't want to deal with her so he pressed the ignore button. Seconds later the phone rang again and Michael ignored the call again. The third time his mother called Michael knew he had to answer or turn the damn thing off. He chose to answer.

"Good afternoon Mother," he said while trying to appear happy to speak with her.

"Do not pretend I am a fool. We both know you just ignored my calls twice. Please let that be the last time you make that mistake."

"Yes mother," Michael replied without hiding his irritation. "Look, Mom, I'm kind of in the middle of something. Can I give you a call later?"

"No you cannot give me a call later. I need to speak with you now. If I needed you later I would have called later."

Michael held his breath as his mother verbally chastised him. He longed to ask her what could be so urgent since she was wasting time berating him, but he knew better. When she finally seemed to get to the point, he tuned back in to the conversation.

"Your father has been admitted to the hospital. You need to get here as soon as possible. The three of us need to have a conversation while he is weak enough not to interrupt."

"Mother, that was low…even for you."

"Facts are facts Michael. Every time I attempt to speak with your father regarding this ridiculous punishment he is putting you through he yells over me. I have an opportunity to speak my peace and I am going to take it. Now, stop trying to correct me and get over here immediately!"

Margaret Ayers ended the call and Michael sat rubbing his temples. He felt the beginnings of a headache. He grabbed two aspirin out of the bottle he kept in his glove compartment and washed them down with a swig from his water bottle. Though his conversation with his mother did nothing to help his confidence, he got out of the car and walked to the door. Shamika opened it before he could even knock.

"Hi Mr. Ayers. I was wondering when you would come inside."

The girl seemed almost happy, making Michael's heart twist in his chest. He did not want to hurt her, but he had to try to convince her.

"Hi Shamika. Sorry about that. I had some business to attend to. How are you feeling?"

"I'm doing much better now that me and my baby are safe." Shamika instinctively touched her hand to her belly. "He's moving a lot these days."

Michael looked down at the girl's growing belly. He wanted to spare her the pain of the conversation they needed to have, but he saw no other way. With Bart intent on using Shamika's case to teach all defense attorneys a lesson, he had to get her to see the importance of the DNA test. He cursed Bart and his father in his mind for their obsession with lessons.

"I'm glad to hear that Shamika," he said as he moved deeper into the home. "Where is Nadine? I need to speak with you both about a development in the case."

"She's sitting in the kitchen. She was waiting for you. We saw you pull up."

Michael followed Shamika into the kitchen and stopped in his tracks as soon as he laid eyes on Nadine. Her face was pale and gaunt. Her ocean blue eyes appeared stale, almost lifeless. She was ill, of this he was sure. The question was just how ill and how the illness would affect her care for Shamika. He questioned her with his eyes. She waved her hand effectively dismissing any chances of them discussing her health. In the gravity of the moment he mentally agreed to drop the questions swirling in his head.

Shamika's case was first. After he accomplished the current task at hand he'd send Shamika to the other room and discuss Nadine's health.

"What can we do for you today Michael?" Nadine said in a voice that was noticeably weaker.

Michael felt a twinge in his heart. He hadn't known this woman long, but he was becoming attached to her. "Well, we need to discuss the matter of the DNA test."

Nadine shot Michael one of her don't-you-dare looks, but he ignored her and continued.

"Judge Harbison signed the motion to have Lamar's body exhumed. I expect to have his DNA available for testing sometime next week. We'll need to test the baby to prove Lamar is the father. Once we prove that, we'll have physical evidence to corroborate your story Shamika."

The life faded from the young girl's eyes. Her hand instinctively clutched her belly. She dropped her head and remained silent for a long time. When she began to speak her voice was barely above a whisper. "No one has ever loved me. My baby is my only chance. I don't want to go to prison, but I won't risk my baby's life."

Michael wanted to yell his objection. He wanted to tell her that if she went to prison she would never see her baby again. He wanted to tell her she was too young to understand how serious the charges against her were. He wanted to force her to listen to him and do as he was asking. But the look on her face as she finally raised her eyes to meet his made him hold all of his emotions inside. That look...the look that made him want to protect her from all future pain and let her hold her baby like a three year old holding onto her favorite doll.

"I won't lie to you Shamika," he began shakily. "There are risks associated with this test, but the risk of miscarriage is minimal with you being this far along in your pregnancy. Chances are your baby will still be born healthy."

Tears pooled in the large almond shaped eyes. "Mr. Ayers…everything bad always happens to me. My daddy started raping me when I was in fourth grade, as soon as my chest started to grow. He raped me over and over. My mom didn't stop him. She never tried to save me! Then when I tried to save myself she left me. She left me all alone to deal with the police and she ain't come back to find me. No one loves me, no one looks out for me, nothing good happens to me. If something can go wrong, it does. I'm just bad luck, but my baby don't have to be. I'm not taking no risks with my baby. No one loves me, but I love my baby. No DNA test until after I have my baby."

9

Michael sat in the hallway outside of his father's room at Carolina's Medical Center. It was the last place he wanted to be. His disposition was one of complete and total exhaustion. Shoulders slumped, head in hands, Michael sat and waited for his mother to tell him it was okay to enter. He tried to ignore the images that flashed through his mind. A memory of his father towering over a younger version of himself as he lectured about the importance of a solid reputation caused him to chuckle despite the heaviness he felt inside. The old man cared more about his reputation than his actual character. Both of his parents did. He could live and do as he pleased, no regard for any other living thing as long as no one knew about his dirty little deeds. He could lie and bribe his way to a career boosting winning streak as long as he was never caught or attempted to bribe the wrong cop or judge. As he thought about it, humiliating Detective Jennings on the stand was his biggest mistake.

Michael wanted so badly to win the case that he threw charm and normal courtroom decorum out of the window. He pounced on the middle aged detective like lion seizing his prey. He'd forced Jennings into admitting the evidence wasn't logged properly. The detective broke protocol and drove home after leaving the crime scene instead of driving back to the station to log it in, or letting one of the uniformed officers take care of it. Michael knew full well the chance of contamination was practically nonexistent since the gloves were locked away in the detective's glove compartment, but he saw an opening for a win and he took it. He'd twisted Jennings' words and spun a story the jury couldn't ignore. With the rash of thefts of police vehicles in the city, all it took was for

Michael to mention the possibility of someone with a vendetta against his client breaking into the officer's vehicle and the jury's imagination did the rest. In truth there were plenty of people that had it in for the cocky football star, so the implication that someone was setting him up gave Michael exactly what he needed. Reasonable doubt, those were Michael's favorite two words, a phrase he threw at the jury repeatedly.

After the way he humiliated Jennings in the football player's trial, he should have expected retribution. His current situation was a direct result of his own arrogance. As much as he hated to admit it, he deserved the punishment his father gave him. He wanted to remain pissed at Jennings for setting him up, but in truth Jennings was only finishing what he'd started. His ego didn't want to let him admit it, but Jennings actually did him a favor. He was well on his way of achieving his lifelong goal of becoming his father. After months of working in the public defender's office he finally realized his goal was flawed. The world did not need another Bruce Ayers.

What the world needed was more Kates. Kate with her bleeding heart and unselfish devotion to the clients made Michael feel compelled to follow in her footsteps, maybe even lead the way one day. The fact that he felt anything at all was a miracle in and of itself, but feeling empathy, that was a new one for him. Uncomfortable at first, Michael was learning to understand and embrace the emotion. Time with Shamika was helping his cause. If anyone needed a leg up in life, the girl did.

"Michael, you can come in now," Margaret Ayers said bringing Michael out of the recesses of his mind.

He looked up at his mother and for the first time since he was a child he saw wetness at the corner of her eyes. Her normally high and tight hair fell down around her shoulders and framed her small face. Michael's eyes questioned his mother.

"Regardless of how much your father has done over the years, I still have love for him way down deep within me. My tongue is sharp because my heart is fragile. I've succeeded in convincing everyone including myself that I no longer loved him, but seeing him lying there barely holding on to his life broke something inside of me. We talked Michael. For the first time in years we actually talked the way we did when we were young and in love."

Michael sat watching his mother as she dabbed the tears away from the corners of her eyes. He'd never seen her so vulnerable and unassuming. He didn't know what to say, so he remained silent. After a long pause she continued.

"I knew he was sick, but for some reason his death didn't seem real to me. I thought he'd find a way to cheat death like he always seemed to do with everything else, but this is it Michael. After 40 years of loving and hating your father, I am going to be all alone. You know what makes this hurt more than anything?"

Michael stared at her still unable to find the appropriate words.

"He's known about the cancer for years. He's spent the last four years being completely insufferable because he wanted to make me hate him, said me hating him when he died would be better than me loving him and having my heart broken. Just goes to show you how much he knew. Underneath the fake hate I threw his way was a love that will live on forever, death can't even destroy it."

At that his mother came completely undone. She leaned into him, something she'd never done, leaned on her only child for support. Michael tried to figure out how to respond, but he was still in shock. It took a moment, but finally he put his arms around his mother which seemed to push the floodgates of her emotions wide open. She sobbed into his shirt releasing what Michael interpreted as years of pain. For the first time in his life, Michael became the strength his mother needed. She showed him a side of herself that he never knew existed and he loved her more for it. He slowly rubbed his hand up and down her back soothing her as though she were the child and he the parent. His heart ached for his mother, yet reveled in her vulnerability at the same time. He felt torn between his enjoyment of her need for his support and the anguish he felt at watching her cry. Yet another reminder of how screwed up his parents made him.

After a long while Margaret pulled back and looked her only child in the eyes. "Your father wants to see you. I was supposed to tell you that when I first came out here but instead I turned into a sobbing mess."

"You're not a mess Mother."

"Oh I most certainly am. No worries though. I'll be fine." Margaret said as she stood and smoothed her three thousand dollar pant suit.

Michael stood as well and turned towards his father's room door. From the corner of his eye he saw his mother begin to move in the opposite direction. "Mother, where are you going?"

"Home, of course. There's nothing else I can do here and sobbing in public is never acceptable. I'll return after I've had a moment to gather myself."

And just like that, the beautiful glimpse of his vulnerable mother was gone. Hard as stone, take no prisoners, superior to everyone Margaret was back and walking swiftly away from her broken son and dying husband. Michael ran his hand through his hair as he stilled himself trying to prepare to enter into his father's room. After the fleeting moment with his mother, he had no idea how the interaction with his father would go. He reached for the door handle and took a long deep breath before opening the door. "God, if you're there, please help me," he whispered before entering the room.

The room was dark save the dim light over the bed and minor illumination coming from the machines next to his father's bed. Michael stood silent and still trying to get his emotions under control. Despite the darkness of the room he could see his father's frail body. He hadn't expected to see his father look so weak. The man that was always his example of strength and masculinity looked like a shell of the person he once was. He felt tears stinging his eyes but he refused to let them fall. All of the anger he'd felt towards his father over the last few months vanished and he was left scared and vulnerable. He loved his father and wasn't ready to say goodbye to him. Selfishly he wanted his father around when he won Shamika's case. This case was the first one that would actually mean more to him than his win/loss ratio. He desperately wanted the old man to hang on to see he was a great lawyer with a great heart.

"Come closer son," Bruce Ayers whispered.

His voice was the exact opposite of the booming commanding tone the son was accustomed to hearing from his father. Michael moved to his father's bedside.

"I'm here Dad."

"Everything I did, I did to protect you. I know you don't understand, but you will. Dig deeper."

"Deeper? Dig into what?"

"Dig deeper son," Bruce Ayers said slowly as his eyes closed.

Panic rose in Michael's throat as the old man trailed off, but the soft beeping of the heart monitor soothed his fears. His father simply drifted back to sleep.

Must be the meds, Michael thought to himself as he perched himself in the chair next to his father's bed. There he sat for hours listening to the rhythmic sounds of the machines pumping lifesaving meds into his father.

***

A tired and weary Michael returned to his office and plopped down into his chair. He switched his computer on and read through emails effectively and efficiently responding to all pertinent inquiries. Once caught up, he moved to the real issue nagging at him. He pulled up the internet and went straight to Google. He entered the words quickly and watched thousands of responses pop up. He scanned until he found the words he was looking for:

NONINVASIVE PRENATAL TESTING

"Bingo!" Michael smiled as he read through the website. DNA testing that would not pose any risk to Shamika's baby meant he could finally convince her to do the test. He quickly printed the information and shut his computer off. He wanted to get to Shamika as soon as possible so the test could be scheduled right away. Gathering his things, Michael stood to leave his office. Just as he stuffed the last paper into his briefcase, the desk phone rang. He contemplated not answering it, but knew Thomas would be pissed if he were on the other end of the phone.

"Hello, this is Michael," he said quickly.

"Hi Mr. Ayers, this is Tanya. There is a Tiffany Sanders here to see you. She said you represent her son David but she doesn't have an appointment."

"Damn! I forgot I was supposed to meet with them last night. Can you schedule something with her for tomorrow?"

"I already tried, she's insisting she see you right now. Said it was an emergency."

"Okay, send her up." Michael sat back down at his desk and placed his briefcase on the floor next to him. He didn't want Mrs. Sanders to know he was on the way out of the door. He fired up his computer again which thankfully came to life quickly. He opened his file on David's case and skimmed through it. As soon as he finished going over the documents there was a knock on his door. Michael hurried over and opened the door for Mrs. Sanders.

"Mrs. Sanders, please come in," he said as politely as possible.

Tiffany Sanders walked into the office and made a face like the garbage hadn't been taken out for weeks. She didn't bother to wait for Michael to offer her a seat. Instead, she sat directly in front of his desk and waited for him to follow suit. Before he could even sit down completely she began tearing into him.

"Mr. Ayers I don't know how you do business, but where I'm from if you give someone your word, you do what you say you're gonna do. Now I know you're just a court appointed attorney and my son's case may not be important to you because we not all rich and famous, but we're still good people and you have a legal obligation to us. Now…"

Michael raised his hand cutting her off. "Please accept my apology. I make no excuses except I was working on another case, and completely let the time slip away from me. I was on my way out of the door now, but if you have a moment I will pull up your son's file so we can review the evidence together."

Mrs. Sanders sat back and pursed her lips. Michael could tell she was still furious but at least she was going to let him try to make it up to her. He turned his attention back to his computer screen. He'd missed the email from the prosecutor offering a plea agreement two weeks ago. Michael decided to keep that detail to himself as he read through the agreement and smiled.

"Mrs. Sanders I believe I have good news for you."

10

Two weeks later Michael stood in court half focused as the judge read David Sanders' plea agreement aloud. The boy would serve community service and attend employment readiness classes over the next eighteen months. Failure to complete either would result in jail time. The plea agreement was fair given the fact that David had no previous offenses and a dozen or so character witnesses attested to his caring nature. The young man needed alternative means to earn money to help his mother, not jail time. To Michael, this felt like a win, although his mind was only half in the courtroom. His main focus was Shamika's case and the DNA results they would hear as soon as he left the courtroom.

The judge banged his gavel and Michael turned to shake David Sanders' hand. "You have a second chance young man. Please make the most of it."

"I will Sir," the tall athletic boy replied. "Thanks for helping me."

"That's my job, but let's not have to meet here in the courtroom again, okay?"

"Oh you don't have to worry about that," David's mother chimed in. "Because if he gets into any more trouble I'll kill him myself!"

Michael smiled as he gathered his briefcase and turned to leave the courtroom. His smile faded as he saw a man sitting in the back of the courtroom. He'd never personally met the man, but he knew his face from television and pictures in various city buildings around town. What was the chief of police doing in the courtroom? More importantly why was he staring at Michael with such contempt?

***

Michael arrived back at the office shortly after 1pm. He needed to catch up on a few emails before his 2 o'clock appointment at the DNA testing facility. Because Shamika's father was the father of her baby, Michael asked the lab to run additional tests. How could her doctor conclude the baby was healthy with such close incest in its blood? He wanted further information. Something about the situation was nagging him, but he couldn't figure out what it was.

He fired up his computer and opened his email. Instantly he became furious. There were at least a dozen messages with the same subject:

DROP HER CASE

Michael opened the first email and the message contained only one line:

TAKE HER CASE TO COURT AND YOU'LL BE NEXT.

He clicked through the remaining emails and saw that they were all the same. Pissed that someone was actually threatening him, Michael shut the computer off and stormed out of his office. He headed straight to Thomas' office once again ignoring his secretary.

"Thomas I'm sorry to barge in here, but we've got a major problem on our hands."

Thomas sat back in his seat and laced his hands over his belly. "Have a seat Michael. Tell me what's going on now."

Michael remained standing. "Someone sent me a dozen or so emails threatening me not to pursue Shamika's case."

"What exactly did the emails say?"

"They all said the same thing. Take her case to court and you'll be next."

"That's it?"

"Yeah. Should there be more?" Michael's voiced dripped with sarcasm.

"Cut the attitude. I'm only wondering how you knew the emails were about Shamika?"

"She's the only female I have on my case load right now. Who else could they be referring to?"

"Tell me what's going on with the case now. What's the update?"

"She's living over at Nadine's and seems to be doing very well. Nadine has a tutor that homeschools her and she's visiting the doctor regularly. We're meeting at the lab in about an hour to get the results from the tests I ordered last week."

"Who else knows about the testing?"

"Only Nadine and me."

"Ok. Let me do some digging. I'm going to have IT take a look at your computer to see if we can figure out who sent the emails. For now, keep your head down and don't speak with anyone about this case."

"That's asinine advice considering I don't talk to anyone now. I don't care who's behind it. I'm not going to be intimidated into walking away from this case," Michael said as he turned and left Thomas' office.

The drive to the lab was short but Michael used the time to think. He could only think of two people with a grudge against him, Bart and that poor excuse for a cop Detective Jennings. Bart was itching for his day in court, so he ruled him out as a suspect quickly. That left Detective Jennings as the lone suspect. The prick had already proven he'd break the law to get to Michael. Apparently nearly ruining his life wasn't enough. Anger twisted deep inside of him. He was tired of dealing with the repercussions of proving the detective's incompetence. If a war was what the detective wanted a war was what he'd get.

Michael pulled into the parking lot of the lab and spotted Nadine and Shamika walking inside. He hopped out of the car and yelled to get their attention. Both stopped and turned in his direction. Michael noticed Nadine was now using a cane for support and Shamika's smile beamed when she saw his face. He hurried over to them and the three of them hurried inside the lab.

After a short wait filled with Shamika chattering away about everything that popped into her mind, they were ushered into a private room. The lead technician walked into the room behind them and shut the door quickly. Michael noticed tension on his face, but decided to sit quiet and listen to what he had to say.

"I've run these tests personally three times. The results are conclusive. Lamar Carrington is not the father of the unborn child."

Confusion registered on Michael and Nadine's faces. They both turned to look at Shamika whose head was now down looking at the floor. The chattering sixteen year old was silent. She offered no explanation, asked no questions.

"I would ask you if you're sure, but I suspect that's why you already told us how many times you ran the test," Michael said testily as thoughts of Shamika's case started to run through his mind at once. If Lamar isn't the father of the child their whole defense is screwed and he had an even bigger problem. Shamika lied to him. He tried not to get angry but he felt his old familiar friend rising to the surface.

"There's something else you ought to know," the tech continued. "Our tests show there's no way Lamar is Shamika's father either."

Shamika's head shot up and the look on her face told Michael this was news to her, but the paternity of the baby wasn't...more anger.

"What do you mean he's not my father? He's my daddy!"

"I'm sorry Shamika, but DNA doesn't lie. Lamar Carrington was not your father. In fact it appears the two of you aren't even related," the technician said as gently yet factually as possible.

"But, I don't understand. How could he not be my daddy?"

The voice of the scared little girl was back as the tears began to spill down Shamika's face. Nadine put her hand on the girl's back and tried to soothe her. Michael took the opportunity to speak to the technician in private. They stepped into the hall and closed the door behind them.

"You're absolutely certain about this?" Michael questioned the technician.

"Yes I'm sure. I'm sure about both tests. Lamar's blood type was AB. That means any children he fathered would have a blood type of A, B, or AB depending on the blood type of the mother. Shamika is type O and so is her unborn child. Therefore, there is no way Lamar Carrington could be her father or the father of the child she's carrying. Even with that evidence aside I ran the usual paternity tests to measure the DNA markers between the alleged father and the children. The results were the same. Lamar Carrington is not the father of Shamika Carrington or the unborn child. I'm sorry. I know this isn't the result you were looking for, but you can't argue with facts."

"Shit!" Michael cursed under his breath. He didn't want to be mad at the girl. Because despite her lie, he still believed her when she said she was abused. Nadine had even investigated. The girl hadn't been to a doctor since before she hit puberty, and her school records proved she had no parental support at home.

But was she sexually abused or raped? That was the real question. Plenty of children had neglectful parents but that didn't mean the parents sexually abused the children. And if Lamar wasn't Shamika's father who the hell was, and where the hell was her mother? Despondent, Michael left the facility without further word to the technician or bothering to say goodbye to Nadine or Shamika.

Michael headed back to the office to discuss the test results with Thomas and get an update on the emails he received earlier. The longer he worked on this case, the more difficult it became for him to understand. How could someone go through so much trouble to hurt an innocent girl? Well, when he thought about it, Shamika wasn't completely innocent. The test results proved she'd lied about the paternity of her unborn baby, but he was willing to overlook the lie if she could offer a good explanation. He planned to head back over to Nadine's after his meeting with Thomas.

He walked into the building and greeted a smiling Tanya. Since his move upstairs which effectively ended Thomas' mandatory hazing period, Tanya had been gracious and polite, a stark difference from the woman he first encountered. She asked if he wanted coffee or if she could get anything else for him. He declined, but took note of the glint in her eye. If he didn't know any better he'd swear she was flirting with him, but he was still slightly afraid of her so he threw the idea out of his mind.

When he reached Thomas' office he stopped at Darlene's desk. She was smiling and admiring a beautiful bouquet of yellow roses. She hardly acknowledged his presence as she waved her hand signaling for him to head right in. Thomas was on the phone when he entered so Michael sat as he waited for him to end the call. After a minute or so, Thomas wrapped up the call and gave Michael his full attention.

"How did it go at the lab?"

"Not well. Apparently, Lamar isn't Shamika's father, or her baby's."

"What! What did the girl say?"

"She didn't seem surprised about the results for the baby, but she broke down when she found out he wasn't really her father. I don't know what to make of it all Mr. Willoughby. I mean I believed she was telling me the truth when she gave her story of that night. She doesn't strike me as a calculating killer, but what if I'm wrong?"

"Whether she's guilty or innocent isn't for you to decide. That's the job of the jurors. Your job is to come up with a solid defense and punch holes in the prosecution's case. I'm very happy you've gotten in touch with your feelings, but the law isn't about what you feel, it's about what can be proven in a court of law."

"You know I understand that more than anyone else here, but there's something about this case that just doesn't add up. And the emails…why is someone trying to keep the case from going to court?"

"Now you're on the right track. If you can figure out who and why, you'll have the answer to how to defend Shamika. Speaking of the emails, they were sent from an internet café over on Central Avenue. Chances are you won't be able to trace them back to the sender because the café doesn't require ID to use the computer. I have a private investigator friend that I've consulted with from time to time on difficult cases. I think you should get him involved in this one." Thomas reached into his desk drawer and pulled out a business card with the name H. E. Higgins printed in bold letters. He slid the card over towards Michael. Michael picked up the card and examined it.

"I'll give him a call right away," he said as he stood preparing to leave Thomas' office.

"You do that, and try to remember what I said. You're doing a fine job here Michael, but remain focused on what can be proven in court. Don't make Shamika your pet project."

Michael gave a slight nod, but did not open his mouth. They both knew that advice was a little too late.

11

Michael walked into his father's hospital room for the third time in three weeks. It seemed the old man was getting better, but he was still very heavily medicated. On both this visit and his previous one he worked quietly while his father slept. Being near the old guy made him feel more confident in his abilities as an attorney. As he sat going over documents and making notes his cell phone buzzed in his pocket. He pulled it out and stepped into the hallway to answer.

"Michael Ayers here."

"Michael this is Higgins. I got some information for you. Can you swing by my office?" Higgins' voice was thick with the Carolinian twang Michael's mother always hated. In their first phone encounter Michael found it hard to pay attention because the accent was so distracting. He found it odd that people born and raised in the same city could speak so differently. His accent polished and professional while Higgins sounded like he belonged much deeper in the south.

"Sure. I can swing by. What time?" He replied as he shifted his weight realizing for the first time that he was standing on the cold hospital floor wearing only thin dress socks.

"Now is as good a time as any. How quickly can you get here?"

Michael glanced down at his watch. "I can be there in about twenty minutes."

"Alright. See you then," Higgins said as he ended the call. Apparently he didn't know it would be polite to wait for the other person to respond before ending a call.

Michael put the phone back into his pocket and walked back into his father's hospital room to retrieve his things.

"Did you find anything yet son?" Bruce Ayers startled Michael.

"Not yet Dad. I wasn't exactly sure what you meant by dig deeper. Dig deeper into what?"

"Do I have to spoon feed you everything?" A stronger but still weak Bruce questioned.

Michael narrowed his eyes. Yes, the mean old man was getting better by the day. Even facing death he didn't have it in his heart to treat his son with kindness.

"Well it would help if you would at least tell me what I'm looking for. I happen to be in the middle of the most important case of my life, so solving your riddles is not high on my priority list."

"My riddle! This isn't my riddle, boy. This riddle is yours. Figure it out, and you'll solve your case. May even stop it from going to trial."

"What do you know about this case?"

"I know enough to know you haven't dug deep enough yet. When you do, all will be settled."

Michael stepped into his shoes and stuffed his papers back into his briefcase. He didn't have time for word games with his father. He gathered his things and left the room yelling, "goodbye Dad," over his shoulder.

The offices of H. E. Higgins were modest but well lit and clean. The tiny reception area was adorned with three sofas as opposed to the usual single chairs. The sofas were black as were most of the furnishings which included end tables, magazine racks, and a book shelf that held books that looked as if they'd never been read. There was no receptionist behind the L-shaped black desk, so Michael tapped the small bell that sat at the corner of the "L". He expected to see an old portly middle aged white man, but instead was greeted by a short black man with a bald head that didn't look a day over thirty.

"Mr. Higgins?" Michael questioned as the man approached him.

"Yes, Michael. Follow me."

Michael agreed and couldn't help trying to guess how tall the man was. He could see clean over the back of his head. He couldn't be more than 5 feet 5 inches tall, hardly what Michael expected from a private investigator. They reached the private office Michael assumed belonged to the investigator and he had to admit he was impressed. The office was very tastefully decorated and large enough to rival any big shot in the downtown area. He lacked a view of the city, but made up for it with pictures that were obviously taken by a very talented photographer. Michael chose to start the conversation there.

"These are some great shots of the city. Where did you find them?"

"I took them myself," Higgins said with all the warmth of an ice cube.

Michael took his cue and sat down waiting to hear what Higgins had to say. He glanced at his watch and noticed it was getting late. He still had to stop by Nadine's before heading home, so he hoped Higgins would stay true to form and be brief. He didn't disappoint.

"I did some digging into the family. As you already know Lamar isn't Shamika's father, but what you don't know is Lydia isn't her mother either. There was a big case of a missing baby out of Dillon, SC sixteen years ago. The baby was stolen out of a car while the mom was inside of a convenience store paying for gas. No one believed the mother because the story sounded very similar to that Susan Smith lady that claimed a black man stole her car with her boys inside but really she killed her own kids. Remember that one?"

Michael fought the urge to roll his eyes at the weird veer off course. "Yes, I remember the story."

"Well anyhow, when no evidence could be found to support the whole baby snatching claim, folks assumed Syreeta, that's her name by the way, Syreeta Hines. Folks assumed she was lying. The D.A. down there charged her and she was convicted of murdering her baby even though they never found a body or even any blood evidence."

"What kind of justice is that?"

"It's called small town justice. When you live in a town that small public opinion is just as good as a guilty verdict."

Michael shook his head in disgust. "What does this story have to do with my case?"

"I think Syreeta Hines may be Shamika's birth mother and Shamika is the baby that was stolen sixteen years ago."

Michael couldn't believe his ears. The whole thing sounded so bizarre and unbelievable, but he was desperate. If there was any truth to what Higgins was saying, he had to use it to win Shamika's case. "Where is Syreeta now?"

"She lives here in Charlotte actually. Moved here two years ago when she was released from prison. Works as a maid for a hotel off of I-85."

"And how are you so sure this person is Shamika's mother?"

"Actually, I'm not sure, but take a look at this." Higgins reached into his desk and pulled out a picture. He handed it to Michael whose mouth instantly dropped. There was no mistaking the almond shaped eyes, and smooth dark skin. The woman looked to be Shamika's twin only twenty or so years older. Michael shook his head in disbelief.

"How is this even possible? How did you find her?"

Higgins smiled slightly, a smile that showed a hint of something…embarrassment maybe? "I would like to tell you it's because I'm a damn good P.I. but the truth is it was just dumb luck. I frequent that hotel because I work there often. I know most of the staff. I'd seen Syreeta before but she's sort of mousy, doesn't say much. When you contacted me about Shamika, I knew her face looked familiar, but I couldn't figure out why. I never forget faces, but sometimes I can't remember why I recognize them until something jogs my memory. While I was um…working a couple days ago I saw Syreeta and instantly remembered why I recognized Shamika. They have basically the same face. I asked around the hotel, got a little intel on Syreeta, and the rest was just a matter of digging through public records."

Higgins sat back in his chair and laced his fingers behind his head obviously proud of his work. Michael didn't want to admit it, but he was happy. This case was finally seeming to turn in Shamika's favor. "Do you think she'll talk to me?"

"I'm not sure. The other maids say she doesn't say much and seems to be very jumpy, but I guess spending that many years in prison would do that to anyone. I can try to break the ice for you if you want."

"No, I think I want to dig into her case first. If she is Shamika's mother she was wrongfully convicted and I want to do my own investigation before I speak to her. What about the person who is trying to intimidate me? Any news on that front?"

"Not yet. I have a couple guys tailing you and so far they haven't noticed anything out of the ordinary. I'll let you know when we find something."

"What about Lydia Carrington, the one that claimed to be Shamika's mother, any news on her?"

"We tracked her down to Orlando, but the trail went cold. Give it some time, we'll find her."

"Shamika may not have time. She's six months pregnant and facing a murder trial," Michael said with more urgency than he intended to.

"I understand the urgent nature of the case. We're working on it," Higgins replied in a tone that made Michael feel as though he were a pacified child.

An hour later, a tired but excited Michael sat at Nadine's kitchen table retelling everything he'd learned from Higgins in hushed tones. When he finished Nadine's facial expression was unreadable.

"What is it?"

Nadine shook her head. "I don't know if she can handle more bad news Michael. It took me hours to calm her down after finding out about her father...I mean Lamar. She's not in very good shape, and with the pregnancy....I just don't know if we should tell her until we know for sure if this Syreeta woman is her mother or not. I don't want to put her through any more stress."

"Fair enough, but we have to ask her about the baby. Bart is going to jump on the fact that the baby isn't Lamar's and more than likely try to push the judge to set a trial date as quickly as possible."

"I've already asked her Michael. She won't tell me. If she won't talk to me, you know she's not going to talk to you."

"Please Nadine, just let me try."

Nadine gave him a wary glance, but she stood and with the help of her cane began her walk out of the kitchen. Michael gently touched her arm.

"And at some point, I'd like to know what's going on with your health," he said, voice thick with emotion.

"Nothing I can't handle Michael. Now let me go so I can go get this child."

Michael removed his hand from her arm and watched as she slowly disappeared out of the kitchen. A few moments later she returned with a visibly shaken Shamika in tow. "Hi Shamika," Michael began slowly. "How are you feeling?"

"Confused."

"Want to talk about it?"

"Not really."

"Well, can we talk about the baby? We really need to find the father. Can you give us any clues?"

Shamika dropped her head and the tears started to fall. Nadine and Michael exchanged glances but neither said a word or moved to comfort her. After what seemed like forever she began to speak, head still bowed looking into her lap.

"I'm not a whore."

"Shamika no one thinks…"

"Yes you do. That's why you wouldn't look at me at the lab today." Then there was more crying, followed by sniffling. "Daddy says no one looks a whore in the face."

Again, Michael and Nadine exchanged glances.

"Shamika what are you saying?"

"I don't know ok! I don't know who my baby's daddy is because he always blindfolded me and put a paper bag over my head! I thought it was just him, but he must have had someone else there too. I couldn't see. It was dark and my head was covered and….and my hands were tied. I don't know who did this to me," Shamika was panting heavily and visibly shaking. Nadine rushed over and put her arms around the crying teenager. Shamika fell into Nadine's bosom and sobbed uncontrollably while mumbling incoherent phrases.

Michael chose his words carefully and spoke in hushed tones. "Shamika I could never think you are a whore. I think you are strong, stronger than I ever was at your age. I think you are courageous and loving. I think you are worthy of all the love life has to offer and if it costs me everything I own I promise, I'm going to find out who hurt you and I'm going to make him suffer."

12

Michael shuffled into his apartment and headed straight for the shower. The need to wash the long day away overshadowed the growling of his stomach. He replayed the entire day as he stood under the hot stream. He looked for angles to win Shamika's case, but even with the kidnapping theory in the works, he still needed to find the real father of the baby. He had to give the jury an answer for that or Bart would paint his own picture. The fact of the matter was Shamika knew nothing of the kidnapping so it played no role in her decision to kill Lamar. They had to prove Lamar was threatening Shamika's life or the life of her baby. For that, they would need Lydia. She was the only other person that knew of the interactions between Lamar and Shamika.

Michael turned off the water and stepped out of the shower. Thinking about the case did not help him relax. He secured the towel around his waist and headed into the kitchen to get his dinner going. He didn't cook often but he knew how to whip up a great steak and throw a potato in the microwave. It wasn't exactly a gourmet meal but it always did the trick. Just as he removed all of the necessary ingredients and cookware his house phone rang. The house phone only meant one thing, there was a visitor downstairs. He contemplated ignoring it, but since very few people knew where he lived, he figured it might be important.

"Hello."

"Mr. Ayers, there is a Ms. Young here to see you. Should I send her up?"

Michael smiled as he glanced down at his watch. It was after 9. Why was Kate showing up at his apartment unannounced that late in the evening? He didn't care. He was just happy she was there. "Yes, send her up."

Michael ended the call and thought for a moment about remaining in his towel. At the last second he decided to throw on a pair of pajama bottoms, no shirt. For a shirt, Kate would have to call ahead. He threw on the pants and ran a comb through his thick hair. He didn't want to put too much into it, but he did want to hear that tiny gasp she always tried to hide when she was turned on by his appearance. Who knew hearing a woman breathe could make him so aroused? But Kate wasn't just any woman, she was the only one who ever had a chance of having his heart.

He heard the knock at the door. He took one final glance in the mirror before going to open it. Once he did, it was he who actually gasped. She looked beautiful with her hair pulled up into a tight bun. Her skin was slightly decorated with make-up just the way he liked it, barely enough to even tell it was there. Kate was stunning without makeup. He hated when she covered her natural beauty with obvious embellishments. He knew some women needed makeup; Kate wasn't one of them. He allowed his eyes to travel down her body and take in the flirty back dress she was wearing. If her plan was to turn him on, it was working. He felt his arousal start to stir so he pulled his eyes back up to meet hers. That's when he saw it.

"Uh...hi Kate. Come in."

"Don't hi Kate me," she said as she barged in. "Tell me what I just heard about you isn't true."

Michael closed the door behind her and stood with confusion on his brow. How could she come over there looking so hot and be pissed at him at the same time? What the hell did he do? "It would be kind of hard for me to say something isn't true when I don't even know what it is," he said throwing extra emphasis on the "it".

"Don't play coy with me. You know damn well what I'm talking about."

"Actually I don't. Are you gonna tell me or are you just gonna keep yelling at me?"

"Why did you come to work at the office?"

Realization registered on his face, but he tried to quickly recover. Too late. Kate was great at micro expressions and his wasn't lost on her. She didn't pounce on him though. She let him speak. She wanted to know if he'd stand there and lie right to her face. "I came to the office because my father fired me and forced me to work there."

"Why Michael? Why did your father fire you?"

"Because he's a twisted old man that would rather believe the worst about me than admit that I am a damn good lawyer."

"You're really gonna stand there and lie to me."

"I'm not lying."

"A lie of omission is still a lie Michael. I saw the pictures. I know why your Daddy really fired you."

Michael's face twisted in anger. "You saw what pictures?"

"The pictures that were taken of you on the night of your arrest, the ones you and your Daddy tried to make go away. I saw them and I'm totally disgusted.

Page | 224

How could you take advantage of that girl? You're no better than the pimp that put her on the streets!"

"Now wait a minute! I've never paid for sex in my life. What about me tells you I'm that guy?" Michael's chest was heaving up and down. He'd wanted to calmly explain the set up to her on his own terms, in his own timing. It looked like someone took that opportunity away from him and he had a pretty good idea who it was.

"You're a guy Michael. That's the only pre-requisite you need and you're forgetting I saw the pictures! I know you were arrested!"

"And you're forgetting this is America, innocent until proven guilty Counselor."

Kate threw her hands up in frustration. "Stop playing with me and tell me the truth. Did you have sex with a seventeen year old prostitute, yes or no?"

He sighed. "Yes, but…"

"No buts Michael," Kate said as she strode towards the door. Her face held more disappointment than he'd ever seen. He jumped in front of the door.

"Kate please...please let me explain! You listened to whoever fed you these lies about me, now let me defend myself."

Kate crossed her arms. She made no move to leave or settle into the apartment. Michael seized the opportunity. "It was when I was working my last big case at Ayers, Rogers, & Winslow, you know the one with the Panthers player. Well, I didn't see a way to win until I discovered one of the detectives had a bad habit of holding evidence overnight instead of logging them in immediately after leaving the crime scene. He didn't do it on all of his calls, but on the late night ones. I did some digging and realized he'd done the same thing with that case. I called him to the stand and pretty much destroyed his credibility and the chain of custody for the murder weapon and blood stained gloves. Without those the prosecution had no physical evidence and my client was found not guilty. I was a cocky bastard. I was consumed with winning and proving to my father that it was time for me to become partner. I went out to celebrate, saw a blonde that kept staring at me and took her to a hotel. I didn't know she was only 17 and I damn sure did not pay for sex! I've never paid for sex, but when I came out of the bathroom she was getting dressed and the police were at the door. I was set up. Detective Jennings set me up. I would never knowingly have sex with anyone that was underage. That girl was drinking at a bar….a fucking bar! You're supposed to be 21 to even get in there in the first place. Her being underage never even crossed my mind!"

"And what about the drugs?"

"Were you listening to me? I was set up! I've never used drugs except for pot a couple of times in high school. I guess the girl must have planted the drugs and the money while I was in the bathroom." Michael sighed, visibly spent from finally telling the whole story. It felt good to be able to say it out loud to someone, even if that someone was the only one he wanted to keep the truth from.

"If all of this is true, why not just have your day in court? Why go through all of this to try to hide it?"

"I didn't go through anything. This is my father's work. I called him because I needed him to post bail. He informed me the next morning that he'd made it go away. I didn't ask questions. No one questions my father. I'm sure you remember that much about him."

"So as punishment for being so stupid, your father fired you and sent you to work in our office? That doesn't make sense."

"Don't you think I know that? There's something else going on, but I don't have time to try to figure it out. I have Shamika's case to worry about. All of my personal drama can wait."

"Maybe not," Kate said with a weary look.

"What are you talking about?"

"Someone leaked the arrest photos to Bart and he plans to send them to the Observer tonight. Unfortunately your drama will be front page news tomorrow."

"No…it won't. I need to make a few phone calls. Please promise me you won't leave."

"I really should be going. I came here to find out the truth and now I have it, so I'll just go so you can handle this."

"Kate please, just give me ten minutes. I was about to make something to eat before you arrived. Let me take care of this and I'll whip up something for us both. I could really use your help on Shamika's case. Ten minutes…that's all I need."

Kate reluctantly agreed as Michael dashed off to the back of the apartment. She wandered deeper into the apartment and eventually stopped in front of the window. The view seemed even more breathtaking than the first time she'd seen it. She wrapped her arms around herself and allowed her mind to wander back through time, back to when she was young, innocent, and madly in love with Mike. She never used his whole name in those days. He was simply Mike, the gorgeous future lawyer that touched her in ways she'd never even imagined. She'd tried to fight her attraction to him, but it was no use. With each date and late night phone call her heart was tangled deeper into his web. She did refrain from sleeping with him for the first few months, but after the dead body of the student that had been missing for weeks surfaced she was shaken. She was too scared to stay at her apartment alone, so she'd moved in with him. That was the mistake, thinking they'd be able to be alone together night after night without having sex. She'd been saving herself for marriage, but now that she looked back on it, she knew she'd always been saving herself for him. Wounded as he may be, Mike was and still is the most beautiful man she'd ever known. And not just on the outside, his soul was beautiful. Beneath his tough exterior lay a broken boy who longed for the love and acceptance of his parents, but understood parental love enough to want to literally kill to defend a young girl he barely knew. That was the man she loved in college. That was the man she longed to feel inside of her again. Her body gave a slight tug deep in her belly which was her sign to bring her thoughts back under control. She'd survived the last few years without sex in hopes of once again saving herself for her future husband. It felt old fashioned, but she wanted her wedding night to be special, not just another night with a man she'd already been sleeping with. Being alone with Mike was definitely a threat to her plans.

Michael walked back into the room and when she turned to face him she had to quickly turn away again. Shit! She cursed inwardly. Did he look that good before he went back there?

He moved to stand next to her. "I got the Observer situation handled."

"That's great," she said, voice tight and slightly terse.

"I still can't figure out Bart's angle. I know he's pissed at me, but why try to destroy a teenaged girl? And after all of these years, why are we now facing each other in court? He's been an Assistant DA here for what…four years?"

"Yes, it's been four years, and to tell you the truth, in the past he purposely avoided you," she said still not looking at him.

"What?"

"You had a client two years ago that was charged with assault and battery, last name Cleveland."

"Yeah, I remember that guy. What about him?"

"Bart was initially assigned to prosecute, but had his boss remove him because of the personal history you two have."

"Then why the hell is he still on Shamika's case?"

"I have no idea. I wondered that myself, even asked him."

"What did he say?"

"He became irate, which has been his staple lately."

Michael turned and reached out to her, turning her to face him as well. "Why are you with him? He's a complete ass."

She wanted to look anywhere except into his dark all-consuming eyes. She thought for a moment of remaining silent. She'd rather not tell him the truth, but with him staring at her searching for answers as though he were reading her soul, she broke. "It was you. Initially we had you in common. I missed you, he pretended to miss you. We started hanging out and before I knew it we were semi dating."

"Semi?"

"I thought he was sweet, but my heart was never in it. He knew that but claimed he'd wait as long as he needed to. Now that I know what a jerk he is, I'm happy I never really fell for him."

"Or slept with him," Michael threw in with a glint of mischief in his eyes.

Despite herself. Kate smiled. "Yes, or slept with him."

Michael leaned in and kissed her forehead. He pulled away just slightly before saying, "One day, when my life is back to normal and you are ready, I'd like to have you back. I don't want to rush you." He allowed his hands to travel down her sides effectively making her shiver on the inside.

Kate took a step back fighting the urge to pounce on him like the sex starved maniac inside of her was encouraging her to do. She knew what making love to him felt like and every fiber of her being longed to feel him that instant. Michael tilted his head knowingly but did not pursue her. Instead he walked towards the kitchen and changed the subject.

"How about a little steak and potatoes?"

"Mike, it's really late. I should be going."

He smiled. "I'm Mike again."

You've always been Mike, she thought. "It's just a name," she said dismissively.

"It's more than that and you know it. Why do you always try to downplay our connection?"

"Maybe because when I was up playing it you were out screwing other girls," she said with enough bite to let him know she was still hurt about what he did to her.

"I'm sorry about that. I wish I could go back in time and undo everything I did wrong back then, but I can't. I was young, stupid, and drunk but it wasn't other girls, it was one girl."

"That doesn't make me feel any better."

"I know how to make you feel better, but I don't think you're ready for that," he said in that low voice that made her insides tingle.

"How do you know what I'm ready for?" She challenged him knowing full well where the conversation would lead. She admonished herself for flirting with danger but her hormones were taking over.

He dropped the dish towel he'd been holding and walked over to her. He reached up and cupped her face with his hands before leaning down and capturing her mouth. The kiss alone made her breathless. His passion flowed fluidly from his body to hers and before she knew it she had folded herself into him and the kiss...the sweet succulent passion filled kiss, unlike any kiss she'd ever felt.

After a while he pulled back and looked at her. He waited for her to open her eyes and return his stare. "You have no idea how badly I want to take you into my bedroom and make love to you over and over until the sun comes up, but we both know you'd be mad at yourself tomorrow for giving into me. I'm serious when I say that I've changed. You...you've changed me. You make me want to be the man you've always believed me to be and that man would show restraint until you are ready. What I want from you can't be given in one night."

She opened her mouth to speak, but quickly snapped it shut. She backed away from him, this time heading towards the door. "I really have to go," were the last words she uttered before she darted out of the apartment.

13

Michael sat in his car watching as Syreeta Hines pushed her maid cart out of one room and into another. He was grateful for the exterior doors. They gave him an opportunity to examine her without her knowledge. Approaching her the correct way was vital. As he sat waiting for her to clean the next room his phone rang. It was Higgins.

"This is Michael."

"Michael its Higgins. I have some news for you."

"Okay."

"We've tracked Lydia down."

"Great! Where is she?"

"At the morgue."

"What! Where?"

"Here in Charlotte. Looks like she was killed about a week ago."

"Damn! I thought you said she was in Florida."

"I said her trail went cold in Florida. I only found her this morning because I have a contact at the morgue that keeps an eye out for me."

"How was she killed?"

"Not sure yet. The medical examiner hasn't had a chance to start the autopsy. May be a couple of days."

"Do you know if the police have any leads on her murder?"

"Doubt it since they don't even have a cause of death yet, but I have a call in to a contact of mine. I'll let you know when I hear something."

Michael ended the call and banged his fist on the steering wheel. He was growing weary of the dead ends on this case. Lydia was the only connection between Shamika and Lamar. How the hell was he supposed to prove Shamika's innocence now? Pissed and not thinking very clearly he hopped out of his car and headed in the direction of Syreeta Hines. He didn't want to scare her away, but he desperately needed answers. He barged into the room startling her in the process. She jumped causing him to slow down and rethink his approach.

"Good morning Ms. Hines. I know you don't know me but my name is Michael Ayers. I am a defense attorney currently working for the Mecklenburg County Public Defender's office. If you could spare a few moments I'd like to speak with you about your case."

"I don't have a case," she replied shyly.

"My apologies, I mean your previous case, where you were wrongfully convicted."

Her eyes darted up at him with a glint of hope. "How do you know about my case?"

"Well, I must confess, I did a bit of digging. I'm working on a case right now and your name came up during the investigation."

Her mood quickly changed. "Wait a minute I haven't done anything wrong! I did everything they told me to do when I got out. I stayed in Dillon until my probation was over, then came here to start a new life, so whatever your investigation says is a lie."

"What if my investigation says your baby girl is still alive?"

"Don't toy with me. I made peace with my girl's death a long time ago. Now get out of here!"

This meeting wasn't going the way Michael planned. He took a deep breath and tried to think of a way to win her over. When it hit him he rushed back out to his car. Within moments he was back with a picture of Shamika. He slowed down as he approached her and extended his hand. "Here, take a look for yourself if you don't believe me. If this isn't your daughter, you'd have to be related somehow. She's the spitting image of you."

Syreeta snatched the picture from him and stared at it as her eyes filled with water. She remained quiet for a long time before dropping the picture to the floor and turning her back to him. "Just because you found a picture doesn't mean you're telling the truth. I don't know who'd play such a cruel joke on a woman in my shoes, but you need to leave."

"But…"

"Leeeeeeeeeeeeeeeeeeeave!" She screamed as loud as she could and Michael got the point. He reached into his pocket and dropped a business card. It fell neatly on top of the picture of Shamika. Michael wasn't much of a praying man, but he left the room praying she'd change her mind and call him.

***

Drained from his conversations with Higgins and Syreeta, Michael made his way into the 4th street

Public Defender's office. The place was finally feeling like home. He enjoyed working with the eager bunch of young lawyers much more than the group at Ayers, Rogers & Winslow, especially Kate. She was the added bonus.

"Good morning Mr. Ayers," Tanya said with a bright smile.

"Morning Tanya," Michael said as he entered his keycard into the lock on the glass door behind her.

"Want me to get your coffee and bring it up?"

"No thanks Tanya. I'll grab it." Michael was now sure Tanya was flirting with him. She went out of her way to bring him coffee, mail, or anything else she could think of. He was also sure he was still afraid of her, so he kindly declined most of her offers. He headed for the elevators and was happy when they dinged immediately. His happiness quickly faded when Detective Jennings' face appeared behind the opening doors. He knew he should step aside to allow the detective room to exit, but he didn't. He stood there snarling at the person responsible for his current situation.

"Good to see you Counselor. I see you managed to land on your feet."

Michael didn't reply. He was too pissed to trust his own words. The doors to the elevator started to close but Detective Jennings stuck his arms out to stop them. "Are you gonna move to let me out, or are we just gonna stand here?"

"Why did you do it?"

Detective Jennings smiled. "Why do you think I did it? You think you could just humiliate me on the stand, destroy all the years I dedicated to good solid police work and just walk away? You didn't care about destroying my career, so I didn't care about destroying yours."

"But why now? Why leak it to the press now?"

Detective Jennings' smile faded. "I don't know what you're talking about."

Michael laughed. "Now you choose to lie…incredible."

"I have no reason to lie. I've owned up to everything I did to you. Just talked to old man Willoughby, played it straight with him. I set you up that night, but I didn't send anything to the media."

"Why should I believe you?"

"You don't have to," Detective Jennings said as he pushed pass Michael and exited the elevator. "Like I said, I have no reason to lie. Unlike you, I own my misdoings. You should try it sometime. It frees the conscious."

Michael watched in disgust as Jennings left the building. He stepped into the elevator and tried to rid himself of the foul mood Jennings just put him in. When he arrived on the tenth floor he finally caught what Jennings said. He'd been talking to Thomas…why? Michael went straight to Thomas' office. He needed to update him on the case, but more importantly he wanted to know why Thomas was talking to Jennings.

"Good morning Darlene," he greeted Thomas' secretary as he approached her desk. "Is Mr. Willoughby available?"

Darlene smiled surprised at his unusual display of manners, but barely lifted her eyes from her computer or slowed the pace of her typing. "Good morning. Go right in. He has a few minutes before his next meeting."

Michael knocked twice before entering. Thomas' back was turned as he stared out of the window. His view of the city was not as impressive as the one Michael enjoyed at home, but it seemed to be to Thomas' liking. "Excuse me Mr. Willoughby, but I'd like to give you a quick update on the Carrington case."

Thomas turned to face him revealing the coffee mug in his hand. It was white with bold red letters that read "Adequate Counsel". Michael took notice of the mug but declined to comment.

"I had it made as a reminder," Thomas explained noticing Michael's stare. "It can be so easy to get bogged down in the politics and the legal profession in general. Sometimes I need the gentle reminder of why I fought so hard to get into this office." Thomas moved to his desk and quickly took a seat. "Now I know you didn't come in here to talk to me about my choice of coffee mugs. You mentioned the Carrington case?"

"Yes, but before I begin, do you have any more information on who sent the emails?"

"Nothing further that I can prove at the moment."

Michael raised an eyebrow, but continued when he realized Thomas wasn't going to reveal anything more. "Higgins gathered some information."

"Is that right?"

"Yes, he has been a great asset to this case. Thanks for recommending him."

"No thanks required. I want you to win this case just as badly as you do. After what that girl has been through she's due for something good to happen. What did Higgins discover?"

"Well, he may have found her mother?"

"Lydia? I hate to break it to you, but Lydia is dead. Her body was recently discovered."

"I know about Lydia, but I was referring to her birth mother. Higgins thinks Shamika may have been kidnapped as a baby. It's a long story, but I made contact with the woman this morning."

Thomas sat with an unreadable expression on his face. Michael continued. "The meeting did not go as well as I hoped, but I think she'll eventually come around."

"I don't want to discourage you, but be careful here. This case is already pretty bizarre, but what you're saying sounds like something out of a made for TV movie. Baby gets kidnapped and raised by the kidnappers believing they're her parents only to be raped by the father who she ends up stabbing to death to protect the child she claims is his but DNA proves otherwise. Do you hear yourself?"

"When you put it all together like that it does sound crazy, but nothing about this case is normal. A sixteen year old girl stabbed her father to death. Normal left the building a long time ago."

Thomas nodded in agreement and took a long drink from his coffee. "What's your defense?"

"I'm working on it, but so far I plan to stick with self-defense. Lamar threatened the life of her unborn child, so Shamika stabbed him."

"What evidence do you have to support this claim?"

"Nothing yet, but I'll die before I let that girl rot in prison for what they forced her to do."

"One last question Michael, and I'm saying this purely to play devil's advocate. What if the girl is lying? Did she even give you a name of a possible father?"

Michael shook his head. "I won't repeat the story she told me, but I believe her. It's going to take a miracle to find the father, but after all the hell this girl has been through, she's due a miracle or two."

14

One month later...

Michael sat in the chair next to his father's bed combing through files. Bruce Ayers had been released from the hospital, but only to die at home. The cancer metastasized in various parts of his body. There wasn't anything left for the doctors to do except try to keep him as comfortable as possible. With all of the pain meds, Bruce rarely spoke but Michael loved being near his father. In these moments he could imagine his father loved the man he'd become. There was no judgment or yelling, just a man and his father. His eyes misted over, but he quickly wiped them with the back of his hand. His cell phone buzzed in his pocket. He looked down and noticed a number he didn't recognize and almost ignored the call, then he remembered Syreeta. He quickly answered silently praying she'd be on the other end of the call.

"Michael Ayers here."

"Michael, this is Alan Winslow. I need to see you immediately."

Why is Bart's dad calling me? Michael thought to himself as he sat stunned speechless.

"Did you hear me?"

"Uh yes Mr. Winslow. I'm just a little confused as to why you'd be calling me. I haven't worked for the firm in months."

"I'm well aware of your employment status. Nevertheless we have some things to discuss. Meet me in my office in half an hour."

"I'm sort of in the middle of something…"

"One hour then," Alan Winslow said effectively cutting Michael off. "I'll see you then," he said with finality before ending the call.

Michael sat stunned, unsure of the phone call. Alan Winslow never strung together more than two or three words when speaking to him over the past ten years, now he was calling him and summoning him to a meeting. Something didn't feel right. He stood to leave but heard the weakened voice of his father.

"Come here son," Bruce said in a voice that nearly reduced Michael to tears. The sound of his father weak and fragile was almost too much for him to handle. Nevertheless, he held his emotions together and moved closer to his father's bed.

"Alan Winslow cannot be trusted. Watch your back. He'll say whatever he needs to say to get you to come back to the firm. I know you think I fired you because of the arrest. The truth is I was trying to protect you."

"Protect me from what?" Michael stared at his father with his eyes furrowed and confused.

"The less you know, the better. Plausible deniability may be necessary down the road. If he questions you about the Carrington case, don't tell him anything. Do you understand?"

Michael rubbed his fingers through his thick hair. "Yes I understand what you want me to do, but I don't understand why."

"The why isn't what's important. Keep digging, and eventually you'll strike gold. I know I'm hard on you Michael, but you really are turning into a skilled attorney. I know you hate me for pushing you away from the firm, but I did it for your own good. I was trying to protect you. After I'm gone there will be chaos. I don't want you involved." Bruce Ayers' voice trailed off and his eyes closed as he finished speaking. It was clear to Michael his father was slipping into a medicine induced slumber but he had to ask the one final question. The one question that had been bugging him for weeks.

"Dad," he whispered.

Bruce opened his eyes.

"Did you have anything to do with me getting assigned to the Carrington case?"

Bruce attempted a smile that didn't quite happen before closing his eyes again. Michael waited for him to respond, but dropped his shoulders when he heard his father snore. He gathered his items and left more confused than ever.

The drive to the office of Ayers, Rogers, & Winslow was short and insignificant. Michael made the trip between the office and his parent's home so many times he could literally get there without giving any thought to the route. Today his mind kicked around various ideas as to why Alan Winslow would want to meet with him. He thought so hard he barely remembered driving when he pulled to a stop in his old parking space. He exited the car and walked hastily inside, admonishing himself the entire time not to appear so eager. As he walked in the direction of Alan's office he began to hear voices. He stopped when he heard the one name no one in the building should know.

"That Carrington girl has to go away. I told Lamar to deal with her, but I should have done it myself. Then we wouldn't be in this mess." A voice Michael didn't recognize was basically admitting he had something to do with Shamika and Lamar.

"Relax. I know the attorney that's representing her. In fact he should be here soon, so you should probably leave before he arrives. We can't risk him seeing you," Alan Winslow said as the voices grew louder.

Michael searched for somewhere to hide and quickly ducked into the men's room. He walked over to the urinal, flushed quickly, turned the water on and off, grabbed a paper towel and made his way back to the hallway just as Alan and the mystery man were passing the door.

"Hi Mr. Winslow," Michael said in his best impression of an innocent voice.

Alan Winslow turned on his heels to greet Michael, but the mystery man kept walking. Michael glanced quickly hoping he'd turn around, but he never did. From his back Michael could tell the man was African

American, about six feet tall, with an athletic build, but that was it. No guess as to his age or appearance. Michael knew in his gut that man was the key to solving Shamika's case. He also knew Alan Winslow had been hired to keep him hidden. The meeting should be interesting.

"Michael, my boy. It's good to see you," Alan Winslow gushed as he reached for Michael and pulled him into a hug. Michael felt his body stiffen but quickly tried to relax hoping Alan wouldn't notice. Alan noticed.

"Hi Mr. Winslow. It's good to see you. It's been a while."

"Yes it has Michael, it's been way too long. Come, let's go to my office, grab a bourbon, and have a little chat. Shall we?"

Michael followed Alan to his office without another word. Once inside he made himself comfortable in the oversized leather chair located near the window. Alan poured their drinks and joined him in the adjacent chair. He handed a glass to Michael and jumped right into the conversation.

"Michael I want to be frank. I asked you to meet with me because I want to offer you your old job back. I don't know the ins and outs of what happened with your father," Alan lied, "but I know a great lawyer when I see one. You Michael Ayers are a fantastic lawyer, one of the greatest young legal minds I've ever had the privilege of knowing."

"Greater than Bart?"

Alan tensed slightly at the mention of his son, but quickly recovered. "Bart's career is one of my greatest regrets in life. If he had allowed me to help him he'd be one hell of an attorney right now. He's good, don't get me wrong, but with my help he would have become the most feared attorney in the state. He's just so damn stubborn," Alan's voice trailed off as he thought of his son, his only child whom at the moment still refused to speak to him.

"I can't say that I fear him," Michael said attempting to bring Alan back into the conversation, "But I'm not happy to be going up against him in a couple of weeks."

"Oh really?" Alan feigned surprise.

Michael played along. "Yes. I'm defending a young girl by the name of Shamika Carrington. She's accused of murdering her father. Bart is the prosecutor on the case."

"A young girl! Michael my boy," Alan said with a smile.

Michael inwardly seethed at the "my boy" statement. It sounded even worse the second time he heard it.

"Michael listen," Alan said taking a sip of bourbon, "the last thing you want to do is defend a young girl. What kind of witness do you think she's going to make?"

"Who says she's going to testify?" Michael countered quickly.

"Listen, this isn't the type of client you want coming off of the win you had. That football player brought you some great publicity. You don't want to throw that away defending clients that will hurt your reputation as an attorney. The firm recently signed another client that has the potential to make us all famous, and filthy rich too. Come back home and the case is all yours, provided you don't bring any unwanted baggage with you."

"Unwanted baggage?"

"Ummm…I should have chosen my words more carefully. Let's just say the firm already has a full roster of wealthy, more notable clients."

"So if I come back I have to drop my current clients?"

"That's correct."

"What about my father? He was very clear on how he felt about me working here."

"I don't mean to sound insensitive, but from what I hear Bruce won't be with us much longer. With his health declining so quickly, he won't be in a position to speak to who does or doesn't work at this firm."

Anger shot through Michael like a bolt of lightning. It flickered out of his eyes and darted straight towards Alan's heart. He struggled for composure as Alan continued.

"As Bruce's sole heir, his stake in the firm will become yours upon his passing."

"You're forgetting about my mother. As his wife, she will be entitled to his stake in the firm."

"No, your father prepared a will long before he ever became sick. Your mother will be taken care of, but his interest in the firm goes to you along with other generous assets."

Michael shook his head. "I don't want to talk about my father not being here." He couldn't even bring himself to say the word death much less talk about it.

"Ok. We don't have to talk about it," Alan said extending his hand and patting Michael on the knee. "But I still want you to come back to the firm. We need you on board here."

"Can I take some time to think about it?" Michael asked the question to appease Alan even though he knew he'd never leave Shamika or his other clients.

15

"Nadine the trial starts in less than two weeks. You have to let me prep her for testimony."

"I know when the trial starts," Nadine snapped. "But I also know that child is not up for this right now."

"You said that a week ago when we first got the trial date. We're wasting time. I have to speak to her."

Nadine sighed and sucked in a quick breath of air. "Fine! If you must stress the child out with this nonsense, then go right ahead, but I promise you if she starts contracting we're stopping the session."

"She's not due until July, why would she start contracting in May?"

"Do you listen to anything I say?" Nadine threw her hands up in frustration as she stood to leave the room. "The child has been having contractions on and off for the last week," she said as she left to retrieve Shamika.

Michael used the quiet moment to reflect on recent conversations with Nadine. Had she told him about the contractions? He really couldn't remember. His mind had been mush sense learning of the trial date. All he could think about was how in the world he was supposed to defend Shamika when he had no way of proving Lamar actually attacked Shamika. He had no clue who the father of her baby was, a fact he knew Bart would pounce on immediately. He hung his head and massaged his temples with his fingertips.

"Snap to it Michael," Nadine said tersely.

Michael lifted his head and looked into Shamika's eyes. "Hi Shamika. How are you?"

"I'm okay. Aunt Nadine said you need to speak to me about the trial."

"Yes, I do," Michael said slowly. "Judge Harbison has set the trial date for May 11th. At that time we'll start the jury selection, so the actual trial won't start that date but soon after. It's important that we prepare as much as possible between now and then. Do you think you could answer a few questions for me?"

Shamika nodded.

Nadine cleared her throat.

"Yes," Shamika said softly.

Michael shot a warning glance at Nadine. He needed her to back off so Shamika would be comfortable with him. It would be important for the jury to see positive chemistry between the two of them. "Okay Shamika. I'll be asking you questions first. We'll start slow and then progress into the night Lamar was killed. Once I finish questioning you the prosecutor will have a chance to question you. It's called cross examination. Have you heard that term before?"

Shamika nodded.

Nadine cleared her throat once more.

Michael could no longer hold his tongue. "Nadine please! When she's on the stand you won't be able to coach her. Let me do my job and prepare her for trial."

Blood rushed to Nadine's normally pale face. "I'm doing my job! Did you forget she's legally under my care? It's my job to keep her safe."

"Safe from me? I'm her lawyer! You know the one sticking his whole career on the line to save her life…she doesn't need protection from me!" Michael shouted instinctively without giving much thought to his words.

"You may know the law, but I know children and Shamika needs my guidance," Nadine said now standing and moving behind Shamika.

Michael noticed she was still using a cane for support. His eyes traveled between Nadine's and Shamika's. Nadine's blue eyes were cold as ice, while Shamika's dark almond shaped beauties were moist with tears. She was on the verge of breaking down. Michael swallowed hard and attempted to regain his composure. "Nadine," he began calmly, "we're on the same side. I promise to be as gentle as possible while I prep Shamika, but it really needs to be just the two of us. Our interactions will be scrutinized. I need the jury to see that Shamika is capable of maintaining positive relationships and that she isn't the sort of girl that could murder someone in cold blood. The relationship I'd like to show them would be male and female, meaning Shamika and me. If I can show the jury that Shamika is capable of experiencing a proper healthy relationship with a man old enough to be her father, I can show the error wasn't on her end, it was on Lamar's. Do you see where I'm going with this?"

"I see," Nadine said in a tone that let both Michael and Shamika know she was leaving but she wasn't happy about it in the least. "I'll be in the back in the den. Just let me know if you need me," she said squeezing Shamika's shoulders as she turned to leave.

Michael made a mental note to question Nadine about her health after the trial was over. For now he needed to focus on Shamika and her trial prep. In that moment her life was all that mattered to him.

***

Monday

May 11, 2015 8:55am

Ten days had passed since Michael's first day of trial prep with Shamika. Today would be the first day of the trial and he was more nervous than he'd ever been in his life. He glanced down at his watch. Where the hell are they? he thought for the third time in two minutes. Court was set to begin at 9am sharply. Judge Harbison was known to be a no nonsense Judge that did not accept excuses in his courtroom. Michael sent yet another text to Nadine's phone in hopes she'd finally send a response.

"All rise, the Honorable Judge Harbison presiding."

Michael stood and watched the stately judge enter the courtroom. The stern look on his face caused an already stressed Michael to let out an inaudible groan. In that moment he wanted to be anywhere except in the courtroom. He glanced down at his watch once more. It was exactly 9am. Michael felt the hairs on the back of his head stand up. He turned around and scanned the back of the courtroom. Just as he suspected, no Shamika or Nadine. There was however a familiar face. Why was the chief of police sitting in on yet another one of his cases? He wished he had the time to investigate his presence.

"You may be seated."

Michael's attention shifted back to the front of the courtroom at the sound of Judge Harbison's voice.

"We are here today to begin the trial of the State of North Carolina versus Shamika Carrington. We have a lot of ground to cover today so I want to move things along as efficiently as possible. Before we begin jury selection I'd like to deal with this last minute motion the defense has filed. It's a motion to have the confession of Ms. Carrington excluded on the grounds that she was questioned in the absence of her parents and denied the right to counsel. Is this correct Mr. Ayers?"

Judge Harbison finally tore his eyes away from his paperwork and glanced up at the defendant's table. "Where is your client Mr. Ayers?"

"Your Honor, to be perfectly honest I'm not sure. I've been trying to reach her court appointed guardian for the last hour and I'm afraid I've been unsuccessful. I'm sure there is a logical explanation for her absence I just don't know what it is at this time."

"When is the last time you saw your client Mr. Ayers?"

"Last night around 8pm."

"Did she appear to be in any distress at that time?"

"No Your Honor, but she is seven months pregnant and the stress of the trial prep has been getting to her."

"Have you called the local hospitals to be sure she hasn't been admitted?"

Michael closed his eyes and cursed himself for not thinking to call the hospitals. "No Your Honor, I have not."

"Then we'll take a quick fifteen minute recess. Mr. Ayers get on the phone and call all of the hospitals. Admittance to the hospital is one of the very few excuses I'll accept for a defendant not being present in my courtroom at the appointed time. Court is in recess," the judge said as he banged his gavel hard.

Michael turned and rushed out of the courtroom, phone is hand, already looking up the phone number for Carolina Medical Center before he could even get out of the door. It took less than three minutes for Michael to learn Shamika was in fact admitted to the hospital.

Michael stood with Nadine outside of the Neonatal Intensive-Care Unit. They watched as Shamika sat quietly next to the incubator that held her tiny two pound four ounce baby boy. The baby's skin was almost completely translucent and he had tubes and wires coming from everywhere. Shamika really needed to be resting in her own bed, but she insisted on sitting next to her baby for as long as the hospital staff would allow. Michael's eyes misted as he watched the young girl show so much love and care for the tiny baby. Her capacity to love despite all she experienced still amazed him. The baby's chances for survival were slim considering how underdeveloped his lungs were, but Michael was convinced Shamika would keep him alive off of her love alone.

"She's a remarkable girl," Nadine said as though she were reading his thoughts.

"Yes, she is," Michael said as he stuffed his hands into his pockets. "I don't believe I've ever seen a mother look at her child with so much love."

"What about your mother?"

Michael shifted uncomfortably, but never took his eyes off of Shamika. "If you would have asked me that question a few months ago I would have told you my mother's heart was permanently encased in stone."

"And now?"

"Let's just say I've seen another side of her."

Nadine smiled as she followed Michael's gaze back towards Shamika and the baby. "Nothing brings the love out of a woman like the first sight of her own flesh and blood."

"Shamika isn't a woman."

"For all intents and purposes, she is now."

Michael sighed heavily, his shoulders sagged with the release of air. "Judge Harbison is going to call me with a new trial date in the morning. I unofficially requested he delay the trial until after Shamika has had proper time to recover from giving birth."

"Do you think he'll agree to it?"

"It's hard to say, but I sure hope so. I need some time to follow up on a few leads."

"Leads?"

"Yes. For one, I'm still hoping Syreeta Hines comes forward so we can prove she's Shamika's birth mother."

"And?"

"And I need to find out who is trying to keep this case from going to trial. Someone is going to great lengths to bury this thing and I need to know why."

"If someone wants to bury it, then they must have something to do with it, right?"

"That's my guess."

"What do you think would happen if Shamika's story somehow got out Michael?"

Michael tore his eyes away from Shamika for the first time and looked into Nadine's pool of blue. "Nadine, what are you suggesting?" He asked as a smile played on the corner of his lips.

"If the person that raped that child is afraid of her story going public, maybe we should make his fear a reality."

"I don't know. Let me think about it. I want to make sure Shamika and the baby are safe first. Once the baby is out of the woods we can revisit this conversation. Lord knows the press will be eager to jump on this story. It has Lifetime movie written all over it. I just wish I knew how it ended."

16

Wednesday

June 24, 2015 7:00 am

Michael sat at his desk watching the live stream of Eyewitness News on his computer. It was exactly twenty four hours after someone anonymously tipped the station off about Shamika's case and she was already the hottest topic on every local news station. He wasn't completely comfortable with the publicity, especially with baby Adrian being released from the hospital only days ago, but he felt he had no choice. The creep who sent the emails still managed to elude Higgins. Alan Winslow had called him three times sounding almost desperate on the final call. Someone was going through great lengths to make sure Shamika's trial did not happen. The desperation made Michael fear for Shamika's safety. It would be hard for someone to harm her with camera crews following her everywhere she went. Michael hoped the footage the camera crews were sure to capture would be able to give him some sort of clues as to who may be behind everything. He'd talked to his father a dozen times but he never got anything more than riddles and broken sentences. The old man had taken a liking to his morphine as he struggled to cope with the pain in his last days. Michael knew his father would die soon, but he was too busy with Shamika's case to give much thought to his father's death. He knew he'd have to deal with the loss someday, but he welcomed the current distraction the case provided.

The sound of his ringing cell phone startled him slightly. He fished it out of his pants pocket.

"This is Michael."

"Is this Mr. Michael Ayers?" the small female voice questioned.

Michael sat up instantly in his seat. He knew exactly who the caller was. "Yes, Syreeta, this is Michael."

"How did you know it was me?"

"I've been holding my breath hoping you'd call since the day I left you in that hotel room."

"Can you come visit me today at work?"

"Yes. What time?"

"Well, I'm here now."

"I'll be right there," Michael said ending the call before she had time to respond, or change her mind, the latter being his greatest fear.

The hotel parking lot was virtually empty. Michael circled a couple of times before he saw Syreeta peek her head out of a room on the first floor. He pulled into the space directly in front of room 106, grabbed his briefcase, and rushed inside. He didn't want to appear too eager, but he knew he blew any chances of that when he dropped everything and rushed over. Once inside the room he looked into the eyes that looked nearly identical to Shamika's. He could tell she'd been crying, but decided not to question her. In his dealings with Shamika he learned pushing her too quickly could send her into shutdown mode. He didn't know if Syreeta responded the same way but he wasn't willing to take any chances.

Syreeta sat down on the king sized bedspread that looked like it belonged in the 1970s. As a rule Michael never ever stayed in places like this one, but today wasn't the time for his superiority complex. He followed suit and sat down at the small wobbly table that also looked to have at least forty years of wear and tear.

"I saw her on TV this morning," Syreeta said staring into her hands. "I saw my baby for the first time in almost sixteen years. I thought you were playing a cruel joke on me with that picture, but I saw her myself with my own two eyes this morning. That's my Bethany. That's her name by the way, Bethany Marie Hines, born January 31, 1999 at St. Eugene Community Hospital in Dillon, SC. I was just a baby myself when I had her, but she was my whole world. I had so many dreams and plans for the two of us."

Syreeta dropped her head and breathed deeply before continuing. "There isn't a day that goes by that I don't regret running into the gas station to pay for my gas that day. I'd glanced inside the store and won't nobody in line. I thought I could run in, drop the money on the counter, and be on my way, but when I got inside an old lady had walked up to the register. She counted out her money in change. I kept looking back at the car to make sure my baby was okay and I never saw nobody. When I got back to the car I looked in the back seat and my baby was gone. I don't know how somebody could have snatched her that quick with me so close." Syreeta broke down into a full sob. Michael remained quiet, but reached into his pocket and pulled out a handkerchief. For once his mother's insistence upon him carrying one had come in handy. After a long pause, Syreeta pulled herself together and continued.

"I always blamed myself. That's why I didn't put up a fight when they sent me to prison. I knew I didn't hurt my baby but I was stupid for leaving her in the car. Losing my freedom seemed like a decent price to pay. I convinced myself she was adopted by a rich family that took real good care of her, but then I watched the news and they say my baby has a baby of her own and she killed someone. How could my sweet faced six pound five ounce baby kill someone? It just don't make no sense."

"She had a very good reason."

"What reason? What reason could a sixteen year old have for stabbing a man to death?"

"The best reason any mother could ever have...to protect her baby."

Syreeta looked up at him. She wiped her eyes with the back of her hands and asked the question Michael hoped to hear since the day he met her. "Can I see her?"

***

Michael's seat at Nadine's small kitchen table was directly between Shamika and her caregiver. He sat watching both intently. It had been an hour since he broke the news about Syreeta and the kidnapping story to Shamika. She'd barely spoken, only cried softly as she cradled and rocked baby Adrian close to her chest. Michael searched Nadine's eyes for clues as to what she was thinking. He got nothing. Her countenance was down trodden and her eyes were fixed on a spot on the table. He mentally pleaded with her to encourage Shamika to meet Syreeta but she said nothing. Michael sighed deeply and began speaking.

"Shamika I know this is a ton of information for you to take in right now and I wish you didn't have to deal with this, but this is actually good news. You kept wondering how Lydia and Lamar could abuse their own flesh and blood this way, well they aren't your parents. Your real mother, Syreeta Hines has never stopped loving you. She spent years in prison punishing herself for leaving you in that car while she ran in to pay for gas. That's a mistake she'll never forgive herself for, but it was just that Shamika, an innocent mistake. She loves you and wants nothing more than to be reunited with you."

Tears rolled down Shamika's face as baby Adrian began to wiggle in her arms. The fussier the baby became the harder the young mother cried. Michael reached over and touched Nadine's arm causing her to make eye contact with him for the first time all afternoon. He pleaded with her with his eyes. She smiled a tiny smile and stood from the table. She moved over to Shamika.

"Give him here, let me go change his diaper and make him a bottle."

Shamika obliged and Michael noticed Nadine was moving without her cane. She was slow and limping, but she was supporting herself without the cane. As she rounded the corner leaving the two of them alone Michael started speaking to Shamika in hushed tones.

"Shamika I know you love it here with Nadine, but wouldn't you like the chance to start over again with your mother?"

"No."

"No?" Michael was confused by her answer.

"You heard me," Shamika said with more anger than Michael had ever heard from her. "I'm not meeting some woman who let me be kidnapped by a rapist! How could she? How could she leave me in a car? I would never let Adrian out of my sight, not even for a second! She was reckless and I suffered my whole life because of it. She didn't deserve to be a mother!"

With that Shamika stood and left Michael sitting at the table alone. He leaned over placing his face in his hands. That wasn't the response he expected. He thought she'd be happy to meet her birth mother. Now he felt like an ass for getting Syreeta's hopes up. Nadine re-entered the kitchen and gently placed her hand on Michael's shoulder as she passed him. She flopped down into her chair with exhaustion emanating from her small frame.

"You're going to have to give her some time Michael. Her whole world has been turned upside down. She'll come around but it'll take time."

"She doesn't have time. She's still facing life in prison."

"Meeting her mother won't have a bearing on her case."

"It can. If I can drum up enough sympathy by showing Shamika has been a victim her whole life maybe just maybe the jury will find her not guilty."

"You can do that whether or not she meets her mother. You're making the mistake all men make."

Michael rolled his eyes. "What man mistake am I making now?"

"You're trying to fix everything."

Michael opened his mouth to protest but Nadine held up her hand in protest.

"Let me finish. Men have an innate desire to fix things for the women they care about. It doesn't matter if it's a friend, family member, or lover, men like to rescue the damsel in distress. In your eyes Shamika is a princess you need to rescue from the fire breathing dragon. It's not enough for you to win the case, you want to save her from every bad thing that has happened or can happen in the future, but that's not your job Michael. Your job is to be her attorney. Your job is to make sure they don't throw her in prison for the rest of her natural life. Saving her from as much pain as possible and helping her to blossom into a responsible young woman is my job. That's why Thomas brought me in on this. He saw your protective nature coming out and wanted to save you."

"I don't need saving!"

"Yes you do. The world is full of Shamika's. You won't be able to save them all, but you can make sure they receive proper legal assistance. Focus on the case and whoever wants the truth to remain hidden and let me handle the social work."

Michael's eyes narrowed in frustration. He wasn't trying to play social worker. He was trying to help a young girl no one had bothered to help when she needed it the most. For the first time in his life he cared about someone and everyone around him seemed to want to stop him. He stood and started to leave the kitchen. He paused at the door and turned to look at Nadine.

"You're right, I want to save her because she needs to be saved. You're wrong about one thing though. The second I stepped foot in that 4th Street office I became a social worker and anyone that doesn't realize that is a delusional ass, Thomas included!"

Michael left the house and was immediately bombarded by reporters. He'd been successful in avoiding them since Shamika's case went public, but today fueled by his not so pleasant conversation with Nadine, he stopped and allowed the reporters to throw their questions.

"Is it true Shamika Carrington stabbed her father in self-defense?"

"Is it true the girl also murdered her mother?"

"Is her father also the father of the baby she recently gave birth to?"

"How were you able to keep the case under the radar for so long?"

"Did the girl ever tell anyone at school about her abuse?"

Michael held up his hands in mock surrender and smiled broadly for the cameras. He was one charismatic man and his hundred watt smile melted women from miles away. The questions slowed, then halted as the reporters waited to hear what he had to say.

"Shamika Carrington is a caring young sixteen year old who has been the victim of abuse for many years. She took the abuse in silence because to her it was simply a way of life. There was no education on the proper way for parents to show their love towards their children because her abductors made sure Shamika only learned what they wanted her to learn."

The reporters jumped on the last sentence. "Abductors? Are you saying the Carringtons were not Shamika's real parents?"

Michael smiled. "You're a sharp one aren't you? Yes, that's exactly what I am saying. Sixteen years ago when Shamika was just a baby she was abducted by the Carringtons or someone associated with them. She was taken from the back seat of a car while her mother ran inside of a gas station to pay for her gas. Her mother was wrongfully convicted and spent years in a state penitentiary. We've recently located her mother and DNA has confirmed she is in fact the birth mother of the person we know as Shamika Carrington."

"Is that why she stabbed her father, because she found out he'd kidnapped her?"

Michael's smile faded and he inwardly cursed himself for being so stupid and arrogant. Instead of helping Shamika's case, he'd given the public another motive for the murder. "No," he replied sharply, "Shamika Carrington stabbed Lamar Carrington in defense of her own life and the life of her then unborn child. She felt both of their lives were in imminent danger and acted accordingly. Now, if you'll excuse me I have to get going."

Michael pushed past the cameras and climbed into the car. He tried to keep a straight face as he mentally cursed himself for making such a fatal error. In his momentary lapse of judgment he'd made the one mistake that could ruin Shamika.

17

Michael and Kate sat waiting outside of Judge Harbison's chambers. After a mind numbing tongue lashing for Michael's stupid mistake to speak to the press, Thomas assigned Kate as second chair on Shamika's trial. He didn't trust Michael to make it to trial without further incident. Listening to old man Willoughby scream at him reminded Michael of the many lectures he'd received from his father. Thomas' words fell on deaf ears just as his father's had. He already knew he made a mistake talking to the press, he didn't need his boss to tell him or Kate to babysit him. He tried not to look at her, but he couldn't ignore the nearly imperceptible hint of vanilla coming from her. She always smelled so sweet. No matter how hard he tried he could never stay angry with her. It wasn't her fault anyway. He was the one that made the mistake and Thomas forced her into the trial. It's not like she asked to be there.

"I'm sorry," he whispered finally looking up at her. As the sunlight pierced the hallway of the courthouse and hit her face at just the right angle, Kate looked absolutely stunning. She smiled as she tucked a loose strand of hair behind her ear.

"No apologies necessary. I know how much this case means to you. I'll stay out of your way and only help when you ask. Sound fair enough?"

"Sounds more than fair. As much as I hate to admit it, I could use some help on this."

"Why am I not surprised to catch you two together again?" Bart asked as he walked up interrupting them.

Michael gritted his teeth and held his tongue. He wanted so badly to physically attack Bart on sight. He didn't know why they were called to chambers, but he had a pretty good idea Bart knew exactly what was going on. He opened his mouth to insult Bart, but was saved by the opening of the judge's door. The court reporter stepped out.

"The judge is ready for you."

Bart entered chambers first followed by Kate and Michael. They all took seats opposite the judge who sat behind his massive desk sans his dark robe. He looked much smaller without the garment and with his shirt sleeves rolled up to his elbows, he appeared almost relaxed.

"Good afternoon everyone, I'll get right to the point. I have a request here by the State to impose a gag order on this trial preventing both sides from speaking to members of the press."

Michael laughed. "I should have known. What's wrong Bart, you afraid the public will be outraged when they learn you're attempting to railroad a sixteen year old kidnapped rape victim?"

Bart glared at Michael but did not reply.

"Settle down Mr. Ayers," Judge Harbison admonished. "Conduct yourself professionally or I'll hold you in contempt of court."

"My apologies Judge," Michael replied sheepishly.

"Now, as I was saying, I reviewed the motion and at this time I am inclined to agree with Mr. Winslow. We still have to pick a jury for this trial and I don't want the jury pool contaminated by one sided rhetoric. Effective immediately both the State and Defense counsel are strictly prohibited from speaking to any members of the press about this case before or during the trial. Anyone who dares to break this order shall be held in contempt of court. Are we clear counselors?"

Bart smiled. "Yes Your Honor."

"Crystal," Michael said not bothering to hide his irritation.

The three lawyers got up and walked out of the judge's chambers in complete silence. Heat radiated from Michael but he chose to remain quiet out of fear of what he might say. He knew exactly why Bart wanted him to keep quiet. Bart knew if the jury had any clue about Shamika's past, there's no way they would convict her. He knew there was more than one way to get the truth out and whether or not Bart liked it, he was determined to tell the world.

***

"I know what's at stake," Alan Winslow said to the man sitting in front of him.

"If you know what's at stake, tell me why I saw that punk lawyer on the news this morning? Why the hell is he still on this case? I thought you said you had him under control. Make it go away or my lips may get loose as well. I may just call my own press conference and tell everyone about all the stuff I've helped you cover up over the years. You think you'll survive if everyone knows what you and the former mayor did back in '95?"

"There's no reason for you to throw around threats, but let's not forget my hands are not the only ones dirty here. I'd like to keep our relationship civil, but if you push me I will push back."

The man threw his head back and laughed a hearty laugh. "You're feeling sure of yourself aren't you? What if I told you there's an FBI investigation into the legal dealings of this firm? What if I told you the only person holding up their investigation is me?"

"I'd tell you it's my job to stay one step ahead of you and the FBI, and you aren't the only one holding up their investigation. Where there is one crooked law enforcement official, there are twenty. I bought the others the same time I bought you. Now if you'll excuse me, I have work to do."

The man's eyes narrowed and he pursed his lips into a hard line. "Now you listen up, get Ayers off that damn case and make the girl and the baby go away or I'll personally make sure you go away."

Alan was not deterred. He smiled at the man. "I own you. I'm sorry I have to explain it to you this way, but here are the facts. I owned your boss before you and his boss before him. Half of this city belongs to me because I own the people that run it. I'll tell you what's going to happen from here on out. You don't give orders in this office, you take them. Now, as I stated before," Alan said as he stood and buttoned the buttons on his suit jacket, "it's time for you to leave my office. I have work to do and you're interrupting me. If and when I need you, I'll call you. Don't bother coming here again."

The mystery man stood and left the office without another word. An eager Higgins pulled out his camera with hopes of getting a picture of the man he just heard speaking to Alan. He waited for the man to come out of the building with his camera held close to his eye. He waited and waited, but after twenty minutes no one emerged from the building. With the recording device he'd used to bug Alan's office he could hear Alan on a phone call that appeared to be unrelated, but still no mystery man. After an hour he gave up and turned the ignition in his van. He pulled away slowly never seeing the black sedan following him.

***

Michael sat across the table from Nadine and Shamika once more, this time the mood was much lighter. He explained the gag order and what it meant for the case. The prosecutor was scared which gave Michael confidence in their ability to win the case. He laid out his strategy for the trial and explained how he planned to poke holes in the prosecution's case. After an hour when he'd sufficiently explained everything and answered their questions, the doorbell rang as if on cue. Michael volunteered to open the door for their guest. He returned to the kitchen with a nervous Kate in tow. Michael smiled at her nervousness. He wasn't sure why she'd be nervous considering the number of cases she'd worked on and the number of clients she met, but he recognized her nervous smile as soon as she laid eyes on Shamika and Nadine.

"Nadine and Shamika, I'd like to introduce you to Kate. She works with me at the Public Defender's office and she's been assigned to help out with your case."

"Hi," Kate said meekly.

"Hi," Shamika responded softly.

"Well don't just stand there," Nadine said as she stood. "Come on over here and give me a hug. It's nice to meet you. I'm happy to have a woman on this case because Michael here has all the emotions of a rock."

Kate laughed and just like that the three of them excluded Michael and jumped right into a conversation about all things girly. Michael smiled to himself despite being the odd man out. He loved watching Kate in her element smiling and relaxing. He knew she was stressed out with work but seldom gave herself the chance to relax. He wanted to introduce her to Nadine and Shamika, but even more he wanted what he saw now, relaxed easy going Kate. She brought so much life to any room she walked in when she allowed herself to enjoy the moment. When she walked over and picked up baby Adrian, Michael's heart stopped. He knew in that moment, Kate was meant to be a mother. Beyond that he knew she'd be the mother of his children. He loved her and when the case was settled he'd make sure she knew it.

Hours later, long after Kate left and Shamika went off to bed Michael sat sipping coffee with Nadine. The house was quiet except for their voices and the ticking sounds of Nadine's wall clock.

"You're in love with her aren't you?" Nadine questioned.

"Is it that obvious?"

"Oh yes, your nose is so open you could drive a Mack truck clear to your brain."

Michael laughed at the southern saying. "I guess you're right."

"You know I'm right. You're in love with her and she's in love with you."

"I don't know about that part. I messed up pretty bad in college."

"I don't care what you did in college, that woman loves you. Her eyes dance every time you speak. I may be an old widow but I know love when I see it."

"I didn't know you were a widow," Michael said attempting to get the heat off of him.

"Yes, my Bud died a long time ago. Threw myself into my work and never really thought about love again."

"What about you and old man Willoughby?"

It was Nadine's turn to laugh. "You better not let Thomas hear you call him that. Thomas and I are great friends. We've known each other for years and worked on quite a few cases together but that's it. Sometimes what one needs more than love and lust is a person they can always count on. For me, Thomas is that person."

"Maybe that's who Kate is for me."

"No Michael. Make no mistake about it, Kate is your love."

"You saw that just from spending a few hours with her?"

"No I saw it every time you mentioned her name over the past few months."

Michael sat and thought for a moment. He couldn't remember mentioning Kate to Nadine. Their conversations were always about Shamika and the trial. "I don't recall mentioning her."

"Of course you don't," Nadine said reaching over and patting his hand. "That's another reason I know you're in love with her. You speak of her without even thinking about it. She's a part of your subconscious."

Later Michael sat on his balcony watching Kate as his conversation with Nadine replayed in his mind. He wanted to believe Kate's feelings for him were mutual, but he wasn't sure if she could ever see past his college mistakes, or his recent ones for that matter.

"What's on your mind Mike?"

"Who says something's on my mind?"

"The look on your face while you're staring at me."

"You're not even looking at me, how do you know how my face looks right now?"

"I know you. Now spill it. What are you thinking?"

"I want to know why you avoided me all these years."

Kate stilled and closed her eyes. She wasn't expecting that question. "Who says I was avoiding you?"

"Oh you were avoiding me alright. This is a big city, but there's no way we'd be able to avoid each other for ten years unless one of us made sure to remain hidden."

"Don't read too much into it. We don't run in the same circles. I don't find it odd that we never ran into each other."

Michael smiled and moved to sit next to her. She turned and looked at him. He reached for her hand and held it in his. She tensed for a moment then relaxed as his warm larger hand engulfed her much smaller one. "Nadine seems to believe we're in love and destined to be together." He watched her as he spoke waiting for her to protest. She didn't.

"I think you've been hiding from me all of these years because you never stopped loving me, but you were afraid to trust me."

Kate looked down, but Michael reached out and tipped her chin forcing her to look at him once more. "Tell me you don't love me."

Kate remained silent.

"Say it Kate. Look me in the eye and tell me you don't love me."

"Whether or not I love you is irrelevant. What matters is the fact that I can't trust you."

"You can trust me. I'm not the same fool that took you for granted in college. I'm a changed man and it's all because of you."

Kate looked away again and pulled her hand from his. "I want to believe you Michael and I want to let myself trust you, but I cant. Your urge to screw anything with a pulse tore us apart years ago and ironically threw us together again. How am I supposed to believe you've changed when you nearly lost everything recently for the exact same reason I left you?"

"You left me because I was an arrogant fool that cheated on you. I did have sex with someone that set me up, but I didn't cheat on anyone. I haven't been in a relationship since you broke it off years ago. I've been free to have sex with whomever I please, and if you notice, I haven't had sex with anyone since you came back into my life."

"How would I notice that? I don't know who you sleep with."

"You know because this is the third time you've been at my place. This time plus the last time you showed up unannounced and it's been late both times. You've never seen a woman nor are there any articles here that could belong to a woman. No woman comes here except you. No woman even exists to me except you. You're all I think about, the only one I want to be with."

Kate lowered her eyes again. She battled her internal struggle to give into him, to allow him to completely fill every part of her body. She longed to lay beneath him and feel his strength as he gave her the best parts of him, his vulnerability and love. She wanted to reach out and run her fingers through his hair smoothing away every strand that seemed to always be out of place. Her body ached for his fingertips. She felt her face flush as her mind reminded her of yesteryear when they made love passionately and lay entangled for hours as they talked about their future. She wanted that again, those long nights of love making and cuddling. The need to have him hold her won out as she turned and leaned her back into him. Instinctively he opened his arms and wrapped them around her instantly making her feel safe. She didn't know what it was about him that made her feel this way. She'd been held by other men, but no one made her feel the way Michael did. She wasn't ready to admit it, but she knew he was her one. She spent the last ten years hating that she still loved him and attempting to will herself to forget him, but the heart wants what the heart wants, and hers was hopelessly tied to him.

For a long moment neither of them said anything. They just sat there enjoying the feel of being so close to one another. The night air was growing cooler by the second but neither wanted to move or end the moment. Michael felt his heart racing and tried to slow it down but he failed. Kate felt his heart beating wildly against her back and smiled to herself at the revelation. He hadn't been lying. His warp speed heart beat and the absence of an erection told her this moment was about love, not sex. That's what she needed from him. She wanted sex as well, but she needed a level headed Michael that wanted to be with her because he loved her. The knowledge broke her and she turned and placed her lips directly on his.

18

August 10, 2015

Michael sat at the defense table barely able to focus on the voices around him as the last two weeks of jury selection and pre-trial motions replayed in his mind like a horror movie. Judge Harbison denied his motion to have Shamika's confession thrown out, a solid ground for appeal should it come down to that. Michael shook his head, he couldn't think about appeals before the trial even began. An appeal meant they'd lost. They couldn't lose. Shamika could not go to prison. It was his responsibility to make sure that didn't happen.

Jury selection was brutal. Out of the pool of 100 potential jurors over half had been following the case via the local and national news outlets. They were disqualified. Of the remaining, about ten percent disagreed with sentencing someone so young to life in prison so they were dismissed. The remaining group left little to be desired by the defense. There were 36 in all; 20 men and 16 women, with only 8 black people in the group and even less people under the age of 30. After the usual back and forth, Shamika's jury of her peers turned out to be three middle age white men; three white women that appeared to be somewhere between the ages of 35 and 45; one Latino man that had to be at least 60; 2 black women- one young and one that looked somewhere around 50; 2 black men both of which looked to be somewhere in their thirties, and one very young looking Asian woman. The alternates were one white man and one white woman both middle aged.

Michael's stomach was still turning somersaults every time he thought of the crew. On the one hand he liked that the jury held more women than men.

Women tend to be more sympathetic than men, but it was their ages that troubled him. He'd hoped to have more young people on the jury. He wasn't sure the older members of the jury would remember what it was like to be a scared young person. He wasn't positive they'd believe Shamika when she described the abuse she'd suffered. Nadine disagreed with him, and of course made that point known every time they spoke. She felt the older jurors would see Shamika as a child, possibly their child and they'd want to help and protect her. Michael thought Nadine was being naïve. Not everyone saw children the way she did, through the eyes of a social worker.

"All rise."

Michael's mind was snapped back into focus as the courtroom stood in preparation of the entrance of Judge Harbison. He felt his knees threaten to give way and leaned forward to brace his hand on the table. He felt a slight touch on his hand. It was Kate. He didn't have to look at her to know. She'd been chatting away with Shamika prior to the start of the trial, yet she'd sensed his nervousness as soon as he tensed up. Her touch helped to calm him slightly. He closed his eyes and took in a slow deep breath. When he opened them he was ready for war.

***

Nadine, Kate, Shamika, and Michael sat at Nadine's kitchen table enjoying dinner like a close knit family. Day one of the trial had gone as expected, opening arguments were presented and the prosecution called their first two witnesses, the detectives that worked Lamar's crime scene and interrogated Shamika. Both gave solid testimonies, but Michael was able to get them both to admit Shamika appeared frightened when they interviewed her, a win as far as he was concerned. He had a delicate dance planned for this trial, one in which everyone played into his hands and said exactly what he needed them to say to paint the proper picture of Shamika to the jury.

Bart presented himself in the way Michael expected, an overzealous pompous windbag that thought he was the smartest man in the room so he spoke slowly and repeated himself often. Michael hoped the jury would be turned off by his behavior. If Bart alienated

the jury early on, this trial would be his to win.
Judging by the body language of jurors six and eleven,
the only two black females in the jury box, Bart
already succeeded in turning them both against him.
Michael watched as the women tried to hide their
dislike but he knew women well enough to know
those two hated Bart already, another win in his book.

For his part in the day's interaction with the jury,
Michael felt mostly confident. He turned on just
enough charm to get the attention of the ladies
without being overt. He pulled on the heartstrings of
the men by reminding them Shamika was someone's
daughter, a daughter that should have been cared for
and protected but instead she was used as an object
for sex. He tried to connect with the older members
of the jury asking them to remember their youth, the
days when their biggest worry was making it down to
the corner store to buy candy. He watched as their
eyes glistened over at the fond memories, then struck
the chord to drive his point home. He told them of
Shamika's young years of living most of her days in a
basement and not seeing a doctor or dentist since

before she hit puberty. He told them how she was only fed enough to keep her alive and social services away from the house. Michael spent a full fifteen minutes painting the picture of the depressing childhood Shamika was forced to endure. By the end of his opening arguments he knew the jury already felt sorry for the girl. Now during the course of the trial all he had to do was rip Bart's case to shreds, find the father of Shamika's baby and prove the father is somehow connected to Lamar and they both were willing to kill to prevent Shamika from giving birth to baby Adrian. Michael sighed at the thought of it all.

"What's that all about? We had a great day right?" Nadine questioned snapping Michael back to the present.

"Yes. Today went just as I hoped it would. We still have a tough trial ahead of us." Michael turned to face Shamika who was now rocking baby Adrian. "Shamika I know I've asked you this before, but is there anything at all you can think of that might help us figure out who Adrian's father is?"

Shamika looked down at the floor. There was a long pause before she spoke. "I can't be sure but I think I remember hearing my mom...I mean Lydia say something about Kipp coming to dinner one night."

"Who is Kipp?"

"An old Army buddy of my dad's...I mean Lamar's."

"Why do you think him coming to dinner is important to the case?"

"I can't be sure because I've tried really hard to block out all of those memories, but that night when my dad came..."

Nadine cleared her throat loudly.

Shamika glanced over at her realizing her error. "That night when Lamar came down to...when he came down to my room he put the bag over my head and told me to be very still and be a good girl for him. He never really spoke to me before he did his business on me, but I didn't think much of it. I just wanted him to hurry up and finish so I could go to sleep. But he stepped back away for a second and there was silence for a while then I heard him undo his belt buckle. I waited for the usual painful thrust but he went slow like he wanted to make it last longer or something, and he smelled different."

"Different how?" Michael jumped in.

"Like....not like cigarettes. Lamar always smelled like cigarettes but that night he didn't. He smelled good, like cologne."

"Shamika, how long ago was that?"

"I don't know. I've tried hard to forget those days."

"Think! This is important." Michael raised his voice much louder than he intended to. His entire body was stiff as a board, he could feel his eyes bulging. This clue was the key to solving the case, he just knew it. She had to remember. He had to make her remember.

"Why don't we all take a short break," a soft voice interrupted.

It was Kate. Michael softened slightly at the sound of her voice. He didn't realize he was balling his fists so tightly his knuckles were white. Kate reached over and rubbed the top of his back before speaking again.

"It's been a remarkably long day for all of us. Why don't we let Shamika put Adrian to bed while Nadine and I make some coffee? That'll give us all a chance to take a nice long breath before returning to this conversation."

No one spoke but the ladies all moved as Kate suggested. Michael reached into his briefcase, pulled out a legal pad and immediately began jotting notes on what Shamika just told him. He needed to find out who that Army buddy was. That was his answer! He pulled out his phone and dialed Higgins. He answered on the first ring.

"Hey Mike. How can I help you?"

Michael didn't bother with pleasantries. "I need you to look into Lamar Carrington's Army record. He served with a guy that goes by the name of Kipp. I don't know what his real name is, but that's what he goes by. He either lives here in Charlotte or he visited not too long before Lamar was killed. Think you can find out who he is?"

"That's not very much to go on, but I'll start digging. Give me a couple of days and I'll get back to you."

Michael sighed again, this time it was a sigh of relief. "Thanks Higgins."

"Don't thank me now, thank me when I find out who this guy is. And don't thank me with words, thank me with a check…a big one, with a nice hefty bonus."

Michael laughed for the first time all day. "Alright. Find out who this guy is and I'll personally throw in an extra five thousand dollars for you."

"Cool! Consider it done," Higgins replied before hanging up the phone.

Michael sat back and rubbed his fingers through his hair, a nervous tick he kept trying to remind himself to stop. Knowing Higgins was looking into this Kipp character made him relax slightly. He didn't want to get his hopes up or give the women false hope so he decided not to tell them he'd spoken with Higgins.

When they returned to the table carrying three cups of coffee and one cup of hot chocolate for Shamika, the mood was considerably lighter. Deciding it would be best to end the night on a high note, Michael changed the subject and told tales of his travels to Europe until they parted ways for the evening.

The sound of his ringing cell phone jolted him from his sleep. He grabbed it and answered without bothering to look to see who was calling before dawn.

"Hello," he said, voice thick with sleep.

There was no response, only sobbing. Michael pulled the phone away from his ear to see his mother's name across the front of the screen. A sobbing call from his mother at 2am could only mean one thing.

"I'll be right there," he said before ending the call and jumping out of bed.

***

Michael sat on the front row between Kate and his mother forcing his eyes not to look up at the casket. The last few months had changed his view of his father entirely. The man he once thought of as an egotistical windbag was now one he wished he'd had more time with. Sure he still wished his father would have just given him the information he needed rather than watch him run around for months trying to solve riddles, but he was beginning to understand the purpose of it all. His father had known about the cancer for a while. The tough love routine had all been Bruce's way of preparing Michael for life after his death, for the days when he'd have no choice but to figure things out on his own. In truth, the tough love was the greatest most valuable lesson Bruce had ever given his son and the thought of it reduced Michael to tears.

Kate placed her hand on his knee. Her silent show of support caused another round of shoulder heaving sobs to rip through him. There was no sound, only shaking and tears as he allowed the grief to pour out of him. He felt his mother rest her hand on his other knee. There it was, the love he'd been looking for from her for years. She didn't have to say a word or try to wrap him in her arms as some other mothers would do. This small gesture meant more to him than anyone would ever know. For the first time in his life Michael felt support from both sides.

Following the funeral, which Michael barely paid attention to, there was the usual gathering at the family home. Michael sat nursing a single malt scotch as the guests mingled and told stories of their interactions with Bruce. He laughed to himself at the hypocrisy of it all. Most of the men there were old business partners or clients. They dealt with his father out of obligation, not because they wanted to do so. The remaining guests were there out of obligation to his mother who had her own way of making sure people did what she wanted. Her name carried a lot of weight in the influential circles. Politicians with hopes of running for city or state offices made sure to stay in her good graces. Between his mother and father, there were now more than one hundred people milling about their home, none of which gave a damn about his father.

Just as he felt his anger begin to rise a familiar voice caught his attention.

"Oh there you are! I was looking everywhere for you."

Michael turned to see Voncelle approaching him wearing the same smile that comforted him throughout his entire childhood. The sight of her made him relax. He stood to greet her with a hug. She held him a little longer than normal, then took his hand as she released the embrace.

"Come with me, I have something for you."

Michael followed Voncelle through the throng of people and into the hallway. They walked for a moment before he stopped. He realized where she was taking him and he wasn't ready to go. She stopped as well and turned to face him.

"I know you think you're not ready, but this is very important. Your father gave me specific instructions and made me promise to bring you in here tonight, so stop fighting and come on."

"I can't," he whispered trying to choke back the tears that were causing the lump in his throat.

"Yes you can. Gone head and cry if you need to, but you gotta keep moving. We need to get inside before anyone sees us."

Michael's interest was piqued. Why did they have to sneak into his father's study? He started moving again and in no time they were inside. Voncelle locked the door behind them and told Michael to have a seat. She reached into the pocket of her freshly pressed apron and pulled out a small key.

"Your father gave this to me a few days before he passed on. He knew his time was short so he asked me to help him get some things in place before time ran out. I've done everything else he asked me to do. Giving you this key is my last duty." She reached out and Michael opened his hand to receive the key.

"I don't understand. What does this key open?"

"Your father's desk. There are instructions in there for you. He insisted you must read them all tonight."

"This doesn't make any sense. Why would my father need to leave me instructions? He has a will in place already. And why the secrecy?"

"I don't know. It wasn't my job to ask questions. I did as he asked. Now, please go on over there and open up that desk. You need to read everything he's given you then we are to leave it here and lock up the office. I'm the only one that has a key and your mother doesn't know that so don't tell her. She'll be tearing the house apart looking for the key but your father said I must make sure she stays out of this study until everything unfolds."

"Until what unfolds? What is going on?"

"Go open that desk and find out."

Michael's feet felt weighted down as he slowly walked towards his father's massive mahogany desk. When he reached the desk he used the key to unlock the center drawer. Once opened he saw an envelope with his name neatly printed at the center. He opened the envelope and retrieved the letter. After the second sentence he nearly fell over. He found his father's chair and tumbled down into it out of fear his legs wouldn't be able to hold him much longer. His eyes roamed the letter quickly unable to believe what they were reading. Not only was his father brilliant in life, it appeared he would be brilliant after death as well. Within 48 hours, Bruce Ayers would become a household name.

19

Michael sat at his breakfast counter watching the video of his father on CNN. It had been four days since the Bruce Ayers master puppeteer show had begun and there were no signs of it slowing down anytime soon. Michael wasn't the only one Bruce was trying to teach life lessons. Countless former business associates were now learning harsh lessons from the grave. It appears his father spent the last two years of his life videotaping meetings he held with businessmen he felt needed to clean up their act. Bruce was known as a no nonsense type of guy so his direct questions must not have worried most because there they were in full color confessing to a host of criminal activity. Bruce made sure all the major news outlets received copies of the videos. There were all sorts of crimes from tax evasion to embezzlement to spousal abuse. You name it, Bruce found a man to confront about it. He'd warned them all about their illegal and unfair business practices and now he was making them all pay.

The best and perhaps most alarming of all of the revelations was the Ayers, Rogers, & Winslow scandal. Prior to his firing Michael, Bruce figured out the other two partners of the firm had been cooking the books and laundering money. He'd confronted Alan Winslow about his findings, but Alan being the jerk he is, dared Bruce to ruin the firm he'd worked so hard to build. Even though the three of them founded Ayers, Rogers & Winslow together, the law firm was Bruce's baby. It was the legacy he hoped to leave to his son. Once Bruce learned his partners were crooked and had no intentions of going straight, he sent an anonymous tip to the FBI. The tip made its way back to Alan which led to a heated argument that Bruce captured on video. The video was now

playing on Michael's television. For months Bruce
Ayers stayed quiet and collected evidence. Now that
he was gone, the secrets were out and both Rogers
and Winslow lost their stakes to the law firm based on
their own contracts. All partner contracts held a
clause that states anyone convicted of a felony in
conjunction with the business dealings of the law firm
forfeits his rights to any future holdings. In short,
Michael was now the sole owner of Ayers, Rogers &
Winslow. The firm would suffer a huge financial loss
from the scandal and FBI seizure of funds Bruce
Ayers was so careful to outline for them. Michael
would still have to settle up financially with Rogers &
Winslow. Even though they lost all future holdings,
their shares still had to be purchased from them.
Michael estimated the law firm, which he planned to
promptly rename, would still be worth around
twenty-five million dollars. That would be more than
enough for him to rebuild the practice into something
his father would have been proud of.

Now that everything was out in the open, Michael felt
terrible for accusing his father of being crooked. It

was no secret that additional hours were billed to clients, he assumed his father was in on it. Bruce never bothered to defend himself or correct Michael's accusations. It hurt Michael to think of how his words must have hurt his father. The proof was now out for the world to see, Bruce Ayers was mostly an honorable man. He had a thing for younger women, but all of his business dealings were legal and ethical.

Michael's cell phone rang interrupting the Bruce Ayers' show. He feared it was his mother who of course was having an absolute conniption over the scandal. When he looked at the phone he was relieved to see Higgins' name on the screen. The judge had granted him a few days to handle his father's death but they were due back in court later that day so he needed to know if Higgins had uncovered anything about Kipp.

"Tell me something good Higgins."

"Well, I have the info, but I can't say that it's good."

"What is it?"

"Not over the phone. How soon can you get to my office?"

"I can be there in about an hour."

"Cool. See you then."

Michael ended the call, downed the last of the juice he'd been drinking, and rushed to his room to get dressed. This was the best news he'd received in a long time.

Michael arrived at Higgins' office a little earlier than expected. He entered the office and yelled out for Higgins. There was no reply. He yelled out again.

"Hey Higgins you back there?"

Still no reply. Michael walked down the hall and stopped as soon as he reached Higgins' private office. He didn't bother entering. He reached into his pocket and pulled out his cell phone. He called the last person he should be calling at a time like this, but he seemed to be operating on auto pilot.

"Hello," the caller answered on the second ring.

"I know it's strange, me calling you, but something has come up and I need to speak with you as soon as possible."

The person on the other end of the line laughed. "You're right, it's very strange and unless you have something that can repair the damage you did to my career, you can forget this phone call ever happened."

"What if I told you I just walked in on a dead body?"

"Why do I care about that?"

"The victim is clutching a picture of the chief of police."

"Text me the address," he said before ending the call.

Michael sighed and dropped his head. He wanted to go into Higgins' office and snoop around, find out what Higgins had found out, but he knew better. This was a crime scene and the last thing he needed was his DNA anywhere near it. He turned and walked back to the lobby and waited.

It took thirty minutes for Detective Jennings to arrive with two uniformed officers in tow. He motioned for the two of them to remain by the front door while he and Michael walked back towards the crime scene.

"Who's the dead guy?"

"A private investigator I hired to help me with the Carrington case."

"Did anyone know you were scheduled to meet him here today?"

"No. I didn't even know. He called me this morning and said he had some information that I needed to come see. When I got here I found him like this."

"Did you touch him?"

"No."

"Then how did you know he was dead?"

"Doesn't he look dead?"

"Looks can be deceiving," Jennings said as he walked over to Higgins and checked his pulse. "It's faint, but he has a pulse."

Detective Jennings sprang into full life saving mode. He radioed in for the paramedics and began talking to Higgins. Michael stood stunned. He'd been so concerned about not contaminating the crime scene with his DNA that he never checked Higgins to see if he was still alive. The thirty minutes between the time he found him and Jennings' arrival could be the difference between whether Higgins lived or died. If he died Michael would never forgive himself. Even though he could feel himself slipping away to his thoughts, Michael caught a glimpse of Jennings removing the chief of police's picture from Higgins' hands and slipping it into his pocket.

"Hey," Michael yelled as he stepped towards Jennings. "What are you doing with that? That's evidence!"

"I know its evidence," Jennings hissed. "Lower your voice. Think about this Michael. Why would Higgins, a private investigator have this picture in his hands when he knew you'd be coming to see him? It's a clue Michael. He's trying to tell us something."

"Us? You mean he's trying to tell me something. He doesn't even know you."

"No. He doesn't but you called me here. You put me in this. Now we have to figure out what the hell is going on."

"Are you kidding me? I wouldn't even be in this mess if it weren't for you," Michael said incredulously.

"Look. You screwed me over and I screwed you over back. We're even. Now if you didn't want me involved you shouldn't have called me. I didn't ask for this. I don't need this shit in my life. I've got an ex-wife that aggravates the hell out of me, a partner that likes nose candy, and a crazy baby mama that likes to pop up out of nowhere with my screaming kid. I don't need any more complications in my life, but since I ran over here like an idiot I'm knee deep in your shit."

"What are you talking about? It's a gunshot. Don't you see those all the time?"

"Please tell me you're not really this stupid, because I had more faith in you than this."

"Say what the hell you're trying to say and stop speaking in riddles," Michael said in exasperation.

"I can't believe I have to spell this out for you! The fucking chief of police is involved in your case. Why do you think he was holding the picture? Whatever is going on here is big and no one needs to know about it except you and me until we get it figured out."

Realization dawned on Michael as the weight of Jennings' words settled on him. How the hell was the chief of police tied to his case? His cell phone rang once again pulling him out of his mental trance. He fished it out of his pocket and answered it.

"Hello."

"Michael, where the hell are you? Court is about to start in ten minutes!"

"Shit! Start without me, I'm on my way."

"How am I supposed to start without you? I don't have any of your notes," Kate said with a tint of fear in her voice.

Michael was surprised. Kate was a brilliant attorney. She had nothing to fear. "Bart is going to call his expert today. Remember the guy from the deposition that said Lamar was backing away from Shamika when she stabbed him? You can destroy that guy on the stand. Just listen very closely to everything he says and find the hole. There's gotta be one because Shamika was defending herself, right?"

"Right! I'll do my best, but what do I tell the judge about you not being here yet?"

"Tell him I was unavoidably detained assisting the police, but I am on my way now and that you're prepared to begin without me."

"Assisting the police? Why the hell would I lie to the judge? Are you trying to get me thrown in jail?"

"It's not a lie. I'll explain later," Michael said as he ended the call and prepared to leave.

Jennings grabbed his arm. "Look man we can't tell anyone about this. Whatever is going on is likely to get us killed if whoever did this finds out about the picture."

"I was slow to catch on, but I got it now. I have a plan."

"What do you mean you have a plan?"

"Exactly what I said, I have a plan to solve all of this. Trust me."

20

Michael entered the courtroom just in time to watch Kate in action. She was brilliant and it didn't take long before the State's expert was admitting there were multiple clues suggesting Lamar was moving forward with only one suggesting he was retreating. Michael realized in that moment that he should utilize Kate more during the trial. Her unassuming demeanor seemed to win the jury over. Watching her work made him smile. She was beautiful and she was his. When they got the acquittal he'd make sure she knew she'd be his forever.

Most of the day went as expected. Bart called useless witnesses, Michael ripped them to pieces on cross examination. He was confident until Bart called his final witness of the day, Anson Taylor, a neighbor that was not on the witness list.

"Objection!" Michael stood and yelled. "Your Honor the defense has been given no prior notice of this witness."

"Your Honor, this witness just stepped forward this morning with some information this court should hear."

"Both of you approach the bench," the judge instructed.

Both men did as they were told. Judge Harbison leaned in close. "Mr. Winslow, what is the nature of this witness' testimony?"

"Your Honor, Mr. Taylor lived next door to the Carringtons for fifteen years. He's known the family since before Shamika could walk. He presented my office with information regarding the relationship between the defendant and her deceased father as well as his own personal interactions with Shamika."

"Your Honor, please do not fall for this. This concerned witness could have stepped forward much sooner than now. This case has been no secret. He's had months to say something. Why wait until the last minute?" Michael was fuming and doing a terrible job at hiding it.

"That's a valid point," Judge Harbison said. "Mr. Winslow, why did this witness wait so long to come forward?"

"He's been in Europe for months Your Honor. He returned late last night and learned about the trial when he was watching the news."

"Oh how convenient," Michael said as he gave Bart a death stare.

"Settle down Mr. Ayers. I'll allow the testimony, but we're going to recess for fifteen minutes while this witness provides proof of his return flight. Without proof he will not be allowed to testify."

Michael opened his mouth to protest but Judge Harbison quickly cut him off.

"Do not say another word Mr. Ayers, my decision is final. Both of you return to your tables."

The men did as instructed. Once they were in place Judge Harbison addressed the courtroom. "The court will now take a fifteen minute recess." With that he banged his gavel and Michael practically knocked Kate over trying to grab Shamika's arm and rush her out of the courtroom. As they neared the rear door he felt her slow down almost to a complete stop. Without bothering to look back at her, he tugged on her arm urging her to follow him as quickly as possible. They only had fifteen minutes to discuss what this Mr. Taylor may say.

Michael walked briskly to the small office reserved for defendant use three doors down from the courtroom. By the time they entered and closed the door behind them, both Kate and Shamika were breathing heavily. Michael wasn't fazed. He launched into question mode.

"Who is Anson Taylor? Why have you never mentioned him? How much time did you spend around him? What the hell is he going to say about your relationship with Lamar?"

Michael spouted questions without giving Shamika a chance to respond. When he finally paused he noticed the look of terror on Shamika's face that he hadn't seen in months. Something frightened her. Was it the appearance of this mystery neighbor?

Kate noticed the look too. She walked over to Shamika and helped her into a chair. She placed her hand on the girls back and spoke in a low soothing tone. "It's okay Shamika. You're safe here. I know Michael can be a bit scary at times but he's on your side."

Shamika shook her head. "That's not it."

"So you're worried about Anson Taylor's testimony?" Michael asked the question knowing from experience he should remain silent when Shamika is upset. Kate looked up at him incredulously. He held up his hands in defeat and mouthed an "okay" to Kate.

"No," Shamika said. "Mr. Taylor came to the house a couple times a month. Most times I stayed away from him because him and Daddy…I mean Lamar would drink and smoke cigars."

"Then what has you frightened?" Kate asked.

"He's here."

"Who's here?"

"The man that was there that night."

"What night?" Kate's voice was dripping with concern.

"The night it was different. The night he took his time. The night I got pregnant."

"How could you know the man from that night is here if you never saw his face Shamika?" Michael couldn't stop himself from speaking again.

"I could smell him when we were leaving the courtroom."

Michael and Kate exchanged glances. She opened her mouth to speak but Michael held up his hand to stop her. He gave her a stare that let her know he knew what he was doing.

"Sweetheart, what do you mean you could smell him?"

"His cologne. His scent was strong. I never smelled it before that night. And I never smelled it since until just now when we were leaving the courtroom. He's in there."

Shamika was now visibly shaking. Kate moved closer to the girl and wrapped her arms around the girl. Michael turned to stare out of the window. He closed his eyes as he tried to remember the faces of the people sitting in the gallery of the courtroom. It was useless. He'd been in such a hurry to get out of there that he didn't look at anyone. If the man that raped Shamika that night was actually in the courtroom, he could potentially win this case today. Finding the father of the child was essential to proving Shamika was telling the truth. He drew in a quick breath before turning back to face Shamika and Kate.

"I believe you when you say he was in there. For now, we have to prepare for Mr. Taylor's testimony. After court adjourns for the day we will go back to Nadine's and discuss our options for figuring out who this guy is. Do you think you can handle that?"

Shamika nodded and Michael went into a quick succession of questions. Within five minutes he'd gathered all of the information Shamika's young mind held on the neighbor. It wasn't much but he hoped it would be enough to help him cross examine the witness.

"Mr. Taylor, what can you tell the court about your relationship to the deceased Mr. Lamar Carrington?" Bart was in rare form strutting across the front of the courtroom like he owned the place. He had a secret weapon he was about to deploy and it scared the shit out of Michael.

"Lamar and I became buddies after he and Lydia bought the house next door to mine," Mr. Anson said in a deep accent that sounded more like the Charleston area than the Charlotte. "We both enjoyed fishing and football so we spent most of our weekends hiding away from the wives enjoying much needed quiet time."

"So, would it be safe to say you knew each other pretty well?"

"Yes, yes we did."

"What about the Carrington's daughter Shamika? Did you spend a lot of time around her as well?"

Mr. Taylor took a deep breath before responding. "Shamika was a troubled child, always has been since she was a wee little thing. The girl could throw a fit like you wouldn't believe. So when she got a little older I started to see less of her. Lamar often mentioned her being punished for one thing or another so I never thought much about her not being around often. Figured she was in her room or wherever parents send their kids these days."

"You mentioned Shamika getting into trouble. Can you give us any specific examples of things Lamar shared with you?"

"Objection…that's hearsay."

"Ok, let me rephrase that," Bart said quickly without giving Judge Harbison a chance to reply. "Mr. Taylor, have you ever personally witnessed Shamika misbehaving?"

"Sure I have."

"Can you tell us about it?"

"Which time?" Mr. Taylor had a look of confusion on his face.

"Let's start with the time that sticks out to you the most."

Anson Taylor leaned back in the witness chair and began speaking as though he were reliving the moment. "Well, I reckon the girl was about 12 or 13. Lamar and Lydia were throwing a Labor Day barbeque. There were a few neighbors there and a couple people from Lamar's job. Nothing too fancy, just a few folks having a good time. Well, all was fine until Lamar caught Shamika on the side of the house making out with one of his co-workers' son. The look of embarrassment on his face when he realized everyone knew what the kids were doing was a sight to behold. He sent the girl to her room, but later that night I could hear him yelling at her about how he wasn't going to let her become a slut and how it was his job to teach her how to be a respectable woman. Judging by how she turned out I'd say my buddy missed the mark."

"Objection!" Michael yelled as he leapt out of his seat.

"Sustained, the jury will disregard the last remark made by the witness," Judge Harbison ruled without hesitation. Bart continued with the questioning.

"Did you ever witness Lamar physically abuse Shamika?"

"No. I never saw Lamar or Lydia lay a hand on that girl."

"The defense has claimed Shamika was being sexually abused by her father. Did you, in all of your visits to the Carrington household over the years, ever witness

Lamar say or do anything that resembled sexual abuse?"

"No, but I saw her try to come on to men," Anson said as he pointed at Shamika. Shamika dropped her head and began to sob silently. Bart closed in for the kill.

"You saw the defendant make sexual advances towards grown men?"

"Yep. Sure did. She even made a pass at me one time but Lamar caught her and made her go to her room. I'm telling you, that girl was as hot in the tail as a firecracker and she constantly embarrassed her parents."

Too stunned for words, Michael didn't bother to object. Though he didn't believe a word of what Anson Taylor was saying, he could tell by the jury's nonverbal responses that they were all eating out of the palm of Mr. Taylor's hand. When Bart surrendered the witness, Michael sat still for a long moment trying to think of an angle to spin the testimony. He came up blank, so he stood and blurted the first thing he could think of.

"Mr. Taylor did you ever have sex with Shamika Carrington?"

There was a slight gasp from the spectators.

"What! No. I would never…"

Michael cut him off. "Mr. Taylor, your good buddy Lamar got a kick out of having sex with Shamika and we have evidence that suggests he shared her with some of his friends from time to time. Now, you've sat here and testified you spent lots of time around Lamar weekend after weekend. Are you sure Lamar never offered his daughter to you? And remember you are under oath. Perjury is a federal offense that carries a sentence that could include time in prison."

"I have never had sex with that girl. I've never had sex with any underage girl and I should kick your ass for saying I would ever do something so foul and disgusting."

"Your buddy did."

Now it was Bart's turn to object. "Objection! The witness has already answered this question quite convincingly Your Honor."

"Sustained. Mr. Ayers, please move along."

"Sure Your Honor, one final question and I promise I'm done."

"Proceed but you're walking a tight rope," Judge Harbison replied with a warning.

Michael turned his attention back to the witness.

"Mr. Taylor, as you know Shamika has recently become a mother. We believe the father of her baby is one of the men her father made her have sex with. Would you be willing to take a paternity test to prove you are not the father?"

"Absolutely…"

"Objection! Your Honor, Mr. Taylor is not on trial here and this trial is not about the paternity of a baby. This is a murder trial. What does paternity have to do with murder?" Bart yelled loudly, intentionally prohibiting the jury from hearing the remainder of Mr. Taylor's response.

"Your Honor, Lamar Carrington loaned his daughter out to his drunken perverted friends. For all we know Mr. Taylor is one of those friends."

"Your Honor, surely you are not going to let this case be turned into something that it is not. This case is about murder, nothing more, nothing less!" Bart fumed from behind the prosecutor's table.

Judge Harbison banged his gavel. "Settle down or I'll hold both of you in contempt. The objection is sustained. The jury will disregard the question and any audible portion of Mr. Taylor's response. Mr. Ayers do you have any additional questions for this witness that do not pertain to the paternity of her baby?"

"No Your Honor," Michael replied as he confidently strode back to the defendant's table.

"Mr. Taylor, you are dismissed."

21

Michael sat on his balcony thinking about the trial. The remainder of the prosecution's portion of the trial continued in the same fashion. Bart paraded witnesses around, Michael carefully wove reasonable doubt into their testimony. By the time the State called its last witness Michael was sure they'd won over at least three or four of the jurors. Shamika seemed to be more relaxed as the case went on. Michael was pleased to see her confidence had increased, but he worried the jury might misread her and think she wasn't taking the case seriously. He'd tried to explain that to her, but she didn't seem to understand, yet another reason she didn't belong on trial in the first place. She was too young to understand the gravity of the situation.

Michael's house phone rang. He rushed inside knowing it was the doorman letting him know his visitor had arrived. Five minutes later, Michael opened his door to the last person he expected to welcome into his home.

"I still can't believe I'm actually working with you on anything."

"When you hear what I dug up you're going to be even more shocked." Jennings walked into Michael's living room and took a seat without waiting for Michael to offer him one. Michael ignored his rudeness and followed suit.

"What did you dig up?"

"Did Shamika ever say anything to you about meeting John Kiplinger?"

"No. Why would she know the…." Realization set in cutting off Michael's sentence. "I can't believe I missed this." Michael chuckled to himself. "I must be the stupidest man alive."

"No objection from me there," Detective Jennings replied with a chuckle of his own. "but tell me what you're getting at."

"Shamika mentioned someone by the name of Kipp coming to the house, said he was an old Army buddy of Lamar's."

"And you didn't think of John Kiplinger immediately?"

"No. Why would I think the chief of police would be involved with a man like Lamar Carrington?"

Neither Michael nor Detective Jennings said anything for a long while. They both sat there letting the weight of the situation settle.

"Shit!" Michael yelled.

"What?"

"We've got to get Shamika into some sort of protective custody, and we gotta get Higgins out of that hospital. Kiplinger has been popping up in the courtroom during my cases, and now I'm willing to bet he was the one trying to keep this case from going to court. If he was so sloppy as to leave Higgins alive to leave a clue behind for us, he's probably losing his grip. There's no telling what he'll do next."

Within an hour, Higgins, Jennings, Nadine, Kate, Michael, Shamika, and baby Adrian were out of Charlotte and safely hiding in Gastonia, a neighboring city located about twenty minutes outside of Charlotte. Michael wasn't impressed with the home, but he was grateful Detective Jennings was able to secure a place so quickly.

"Look, this is my baby's mama's spot. She lets me kick it here when she's not tripping, but her fuse is short so we gotta hurry up and finish all this before she flips."

Michael's lips curved into a smile. "You looked stressed man. Relax, I told you I have a plan. Now that everyone is safely in place, I can put it in motion."

"You better be right about this because if not we're all gonna come up missing."

***

"Michael, I'm glad to see you've come to your senses, but as you well know you're a little too late. Your father made sure I was done in the legal profession forever."

"I know Mr. Winslow," Michael said with mock sincerity. "That's why I wanted to talk to you. What if I offered you half of my share of the company?"

Alan raised an eyebrow. "Go on."

"Well, I'd like to prove that I can make this firm great, but quite frankly, I'm not sure if there will be a firm without you. Before the Carrington case, my name held weight but after what my father has done and what is about to unfold with this case...my name will be as good as mud."

Alan gave him a quizzical glance. "Why do you say that?"

"Things were going well initially, but I've hit a bit of a snag that I don't think we'll be able to overcome."

"And what is that?" Alan Winslow was trying his best to mask his interest but his efforts were futile. Michael saw right through him.

"I found out who the father of the baby is."

"Really?" Alan nearly jumped out of his seat, but he restrained himself.

"Yes, and you'll never guess who it is." Michael said shaking his head slowly.

"Who is it?"

"A teenaged boy Shamika went to school with."

"So the girl was lying all this time?"

"Yes," Michael said with his head bowed and shoulders slumped. "I've thrown my career on the line and the entire story has been nothing more than a figment of Shamika's imagination. After this, I'll be done. No one is going to hire an attorney that couldn't even see through the lies of a little girl."

Michael began to bang his forehead into the palm of his hand for dramatic flair. "Stupid, stupid, stupid. How could I be so stupid?"

Alan smiled when he thought Michael couldn't see him. "That's nonsense. As I said before, you are one of the most brilliant young minds I know. It's true, your reputation will take a slight hit, but with the right spin, you should be able to separate yourself from Shamika, especially if you drop the case now."

Michael looked up at Alan with hopeful intensity. "I doubt Judge Harbison will let me drop this case this far into the trial, but if you really think I'll be able to survive this, I'd appreciate the opportunity to work with you when this is all over." Michael almost choked on the words, but he kept his emotions in check.

Alan eyed Michael suspiciously. "You know, I've never seen you so humble. Is there anything you're not telling me?"

"Discovering you've nearly thrown your entire career away on the word of a lying teenager has a way of humbling a man. After everything I've been through recently I just want to get this case behind me and forget I ever met Shamika Carrington."

"I still don't get why you need me. With Rogers and I out of the way, the firm is all yours to build as you please. Plus I know what your father's estate was worth and he left the majority of it to you. You're not hurting for money son. What is all of this really about?"

Michael hadn't expected Alan to question his motives, but he was a quick thinker. "All of the money in the world won't rebuild the firm after what my father leaked to the press. Besides, I don't want to just live off of my inheritance. I want to make a name for myself and prove to him, even if he is dead, that I am more of a man than he ever gave me credit for. I want to take the firm past the level of success he was ever able to achieve, but I can't do it alone. Quite frankly, I need your contacts and connections to bring more big name clients to the law firm."

Alan nodded his head as if to say he understood. He remained silent for a moment and then spoke slowly and deliberately. "I will help you, but you must get yourself kicked off of this Carrington case."

"But I…"

"No buts," Alan said cutting Michael off. "Get off the case or kiss your dreams of rebuilding the firm goodbye."

Michael sat at the table telling everyone about his meeting with Alan. The group all agreed Alan was still way too interested in making sure Michael did not continue on Shamika's case which meant he was still working for the person trying to prevent the case from going public.

"Michael, can I holla at you outside for a second?" Detective Jennings was already on his feet and heading towards the door before Michael had a chance to respond.

Michael didn't bother trying to resist. He followed Jennings outside and waited until the door was closed behind him before he spoke. "What's up?"

"I think this thing may be deeper than we realized."

"What did you find out?"

"My Captain called me into his office today and suspended me. He claimed a woman I gave a traffic ticket to last week filed a sexual misconduct complaint against me."

Michael snickered. "At a time like this you chose to grope some big breasted bimbo?"

Jennings' jaw tightened reflexively. "No, I leave the groping of women to you. It seems that blonde you picked up a few months back worked out real well for you."

Now it was Michael's turn to try to cool his rising temper. "That was a low blow, even for you."

Jennings held up his hands in mock surrender. "Look let's just focus on finishing this case so you can go back to your corner and I can go back to mine."

"Fair enough," Michael said in a voice that conveyed his sincerity. "So back to the suspension, what does it mean for us?"

"Basically it means I am legally blackballed from my usual investigation methods and prohibited from working on the case."

"So we're screwed?"

"Not necessarily. I said I couldn't use my usual investigation methods," Jennings said with a sly smile. "I have plenty of tricks up my sleeve. Cap just freed me so I can use them."

Michael smiled in return. "So I wasn't completely wrong about you. You do know how to bend the rules."

Jennings stopped smiling. "Let's get one thing straight. I've never mishandled evidence or lied on a suspect. I run my investigations by the book, but since this mess you drug me in can't be formally investigated I have to do what I have to do to make sure we're all alive when this is all over."

"Look, for what it's worth, I appreciate everything you're doing to help Shamika. She doesn't deserve to spend the rest of her life in prison when the son of a bitch that started it all is going around doing press conferences and shit. There's no telling how many other young girls he's ruined over the years."

"I still can't believe he's involved. I mean I don't know him well, but he's got a reputation of being very hard on child molesters."

"What better way to cover his tracks than to pretend to hate his own kind? Scum like him make me sick to my stomach. All the grown women out here throwing themselves at men in uniform every day and he'd rather rape a child."

"Hey," Jennings said deciding to change the subject to a safer topic. "Why did you lie to Winslow about the father of the baby?"

"Because I want to see how useful he'll be towards my plan."

"What plan?"

"You'll see. Just give me a few more days."

22

After two weeks of hiding, more mind numbing court room drama, and Michael spoon feeding Alan false information about the case, his efforts finally started to pay off. Sitting in Judge Harbison's chambers, Michael could barely contain himself as he listened to Bart drone on and on about his motion to have baby Adrian tested for paternity. The irony of the whole argument made Michael fight to keep silent. Kate was having a field day watching Bart try to twist the situation after he himself repeatedly insisted the paternity of the baby had nothing to do with the trial. Based on the way the judge was responding, he seemed to agree with Kate and Michael.

"Counselor, you've maintained throughout this trial that the paternity of the baby was not relevant to the case. Why the sudden change of heart?" Judge Harbison questioned Bart with a tone that let everyone in the room know he wasn't buying what Bart was selling.

He's been getting the fake information I'm feeding his dear old dad, Michael thought. It amazed him how predictable Bart and Alan both were. He knew Alan wanted more than anything to re-establish a relationship with his only son, so in a way feeding Alan the fake info worked out for both of them. Bart was an evil bastard. He deserved to be humiliated, which is exactly what was about to happen.

"Your Honor, I'm sure you understand how theories can change as additional evidence comes to light," Bart said almost pleading with the judge to side with him.

"I do," the judge conceded.

"Well, that's what's happening here. The defense maintains that Lamar Carrington raped Shamika and impregnated her. Now we've learned that the baby not only isn't Lamar's, but that the father is a boy Shamika went to school with. This young man would like his opportunity to testify to the character of Shamika and things he personally heard Shamika say about her father." Bart was no longer pleading. He was smug, like he just knew the judge would agree with him. He was wrong.

"Mr. Winslow, you may present your witness and he may testify as to the character of Ms. Carrington. I will not however, order a paternity test. Throughout this trial you have maintained, and I'm inclined to agree, that the paternity of Shamika's baby had no bearing on her decision to stab Lamar. To that end, I will allow the witness to testify but you will not be allowed to question him regarding the paternity of the baby. Are we clear?"

Michael and Kate both struggled to hide their delight as they stood to exit the Judge's chambers. Neither said a word to each, even as Bart threw out his usual barrage of insults. They walked hand in hand in silence until they were safely back inside the 4th Street offices. They greeted Tanya before heading to the elevators and riding up to the tenth floor. Once they exited, the smile was gone from their faces. There standing shaking Thomas' hand was the chief of police...Mr. John Kiplinger.

Michael felt his blood boil. He wasn't sure if he was more angry that Kiplinger was responsible for raping Shamika, or the fact that he was still trying to ruin her life to protect his own. He felt Kate squeeze his hand. He didn't take his gaze off of Kiplinger. She squeezed it again, again he ignored her. She released his hand and stood directly in front of him. Though she was shorter than he was, she could still slightly disrupt his view.

"Look at me," she demanded.

Michael obeyed.

"We are so close to getting Shamika acquitted. Don't do anything stupid to hurt our chances."

Michael closed his eyes. Kate was right. He had to keep his head in the game. He wasn't sure what

Kiplinger's move was, but he wasn't going to let the man rattle him. If there was ever any doubt as to whether or not Kiplinger knew that Michael knew his secret, it vanished the second the police chief turned to leave the office. He winked at Michael and splashed a "your move Counselor" smile in his direction. Michael wanted to do something clever in return but instead he stood there staring incredulously at the police chief. It took three tries for Thomas to get his attention.

"In my office Mr. Ayers," Thomas yelled a little more loudly than was customary for him.

Michael snapped out of his trance and followed Thomas into his office. He took a seat opposite Thomas and waited to hear what the old man had to say.

"I don't know how to say this Michael other than to come right out and say it. I have to let you go."

"What? Why?"

"It appears your secret indiscretion that landed you hear is about to become front page news and I can't bring that type of attention to this office."

"That son of a bitch! How can he get me fired when you aren't even paying me? This is community service!" Michael was fuming again.

"Technically, it's not community service. You were never charged and therefore never sentenced. This is an agreement I reached with your father. I kept you on after his death because I felt you were doing a fantastic job and the truth of the matter is, this office will never be able to afford an attorney of your caliber. It just made sense to keep you in place as long as you wanted to remain here, but I can't do that any longer."

"This is just another ploy to get me to drop the Carrington case. Kiplinger doesn't want me on it because he knows I'll expose him as the child molesting fraud he really is."

Thomas raised his eye brows. "Did you really just call the chief of police a child molester?"

Michael closed his eyes and tossed his head back. He really had to get a grip on his mouth when riled up. "Look, the less you know the safer you'll be. Just give me a little while to collect my things and I'll be out of here."

"You do know this means you'll be off of the Carrington case, right?"

Michael stared at Thomas incredulously. "No. I won't be off of the case. I'm still a practicing attorney and I'll still represent Shamika. With or without this office, I will make sure that girl never spends another second in jail...or I'll die trying."

After spending all afternoon trying to get his contacts at the Charlotte Observer not to run the story on him, a tired and dejected Michael sat nursing a beer with Jennings.

"What's the worst that can happen?" Jennings wasn't drunk but he was nearly there. His eyes were dancing and his speech noticeably slower. Michael made a mental note to prevent the bartender from giving him anymore rounds.

"My reputation is hanging on by a thread here. How am I supposed to defend Shamika, a victim of molestation if I myself am being accused of molestation? The implications alone are terrible but thanks to you they have pictures."

"Look man, I was only trying to get you back for what you did to me, and I never gave those pictures to anyone. I don't know how Kiplinger got ahold of them."

"It doesn't matter now. What matters is figuring out how to prove I'm innocent. We can't let him get away with this. What happens to the next girl?"

"Who says there'll be a next girl?"

Michael shot daggers at Jennings with his eyes. "You've been around enough criminals to know a tiger doesn't change his stripes."

"Yes, but we only have circumstantial evidence on Kiplinger. We don't know for sure that he's the father of that baby, or that he ever raped anyone for that matter."

"We may not be able to prove it yet, but you and I both know he's going through great lengths to keep this thing hidden. He wouldn't be doing all of that if he didn't have anything to do with this. And he shot Higgins when he realized he was on to him! He's guilty and you know it!" Michael glared at Jennings, chest heaving. How could he be so stupid as to think there was a snowball's chance in hell that Kiplinger was innocent?

"Stop staring at me like that. I know the facts of this case better than you. But the law isn't about what you know, it's about what you can prove and right now we can't prove anything."

"I'm not worried about proving he's guilty in court. Not right now anyway. I just want to make sure Shamika doesn't go to prison. I need to paint the picture to prove how she's been abused. That's it. Everything else can be handled later. But I can't do any of it if he tries to throw me in jail for the crime you set me up for." Michael's tone was now accusatory.

"Look, I've said I was sorry but you had that coming to you for the way you tried to ruin my career. If there was something I could do to help you out, I would but I'm suspended so my hands are tied."

"Do you mean that?"

"Do I mean what?"

"Do you mean you'd help me if you could?"

"Yeah," Jennings scoffed.

"Good. Because I have a plan and you're gonna help me pull it off."

The next morning on the steps of the courthouse a bright eyed smiling Michael and a stoic Jennings stood before a throng of reporters. This time wasn't impromptu like Michael's so-called interview in front of Nadine's house. This time he and Jennings had stayed up all night preparing. He was ready to beat Kiplinger at his own game. If he wanted to bring Michael publicity, he'd gladly accept it.

"Good morning. I'm sure by now most of you have seen the story about me that was published in the

Page | 372

Charlotte Observer. It's important to me that people understand that the man described in that story is not who I am. In fact it goes against everything I stand for as a man and as an attorney. The fact is, nearly a year ago I made the mistake of discrediting a highly decorated detective on the stand. I was crass and discredited the years of hard work and dedication this detective has put into his job protecting and serving the good people of Charlotte. As a result, I drove an honest man to do something he's never done before. He framed me for a crime I didn't commit."

The reporters all jumped at his revelation.

"Detective is this true? Are you agreeing with his statement? Did you frame him?"

The reporters yelled questions at Jennings. He stood there quietly letting them all yell. He struggled internally to keep his word. He'd agreed to the press conference, he wanted to help Michael, but admitting to career suicide and opening himself up to his own potential legal troubles was too much to ask of anyone. In the end, he couldn't do it.

"I can attest to the validity of Mr. Ayers' story to this extent...he is innocent of all of the allegations that have been made against him. Mr. Ayers is a decent man and one of the best defense attorneys I have had the privilege of knowing. Now, I was not the arresting officer but I have personal knowledge that the alleged underage victim was actually nineteen at the time of the incident and there is no record of her ever being connected to prostitution."

"How do you know the age of the young woman? Why are you here if you didn't frame him?"

More reporters shouted in their direction but a shocked and angry Michael threw up his hands. "That's all for now folks," he said as he turned to head into the courthouse pulling Detective Jennings along with him. Once they were tucked away in one of the meeting rooms Michael released all of his fury.

"Why the hell would you leave me hanging like that? You gave me your word and then screwed me in front of the cameras!"

"I was supposed to throw my career away to save yours? That's bullshit and you know it! Look you screwed me and I screwed you. You started this shit. I don't owe you anything."

"Like hell you don't. I just called you out on your incompetence. You set me up to be arrested. The two are not the same! And what was that about the girl not being underage?" Michael stood toe to toe with Jennings practically breathing fire from his nostrils. He couldn't remember the last time he'd been so angry.

Jennings smiled. "She's not. She's a 21 year old student at UNC Charlotte."

Michael narrowed his eyes. "You said she was underage."

"I said a lot of things. I also said the white powder was cocaine."

Michael lunged for Jennings, but he'd never been much of a fighter. As such, Jennings stepped to the side and had Michael in a choke hold within a few seconds. Michael tried to squirm his way out, but Jennings had a death grip on him. He didn't apply much pressure, just enough to keep Michael still while he confessed.

"I only wanted to teach you a lesson about messing with me. I wouldn't actually allow anyone to have sex with an underage girl, nor would I plant drugs on a suspect. You were so cocky and arrogant, and then your daddy bailed you out and made the charges go away. Neither one of you great defense attorneys ever took the time to investigate the evidence. You did this to yourself. You messed up your life, not me. And if you don't start paying attention to the evidence in this case instead of chasing rabbits down never ending holes, you're going to do the same thing to that little girl."

23

Michael sat at the tiny kitchen table and poured over his notes. The statement Jennings made regarding ignoring the evidence has been bugging him since their scuffle a week ago. The prosecution rested its case earlier that day. Early the following morning he would begin presenting his defense. If he was missing something he had to find it before it was too late. He'd read everything in the file so often he knew everything by heart but he continued reviewing the pages knowing there was something there, something that would save Shamika.

The sound of baby Adrian cooing caused him to look up and see Shamika standing in the doorway. Her eyes told him she really needed to speak to him. As much as he needed to work, the last few months of his life had taught him to pause and listen during the rare moments she actually wanted to speak.

"Come on over and have a seat," Michael said as he moved the papers covering the table.

"I didn't want to bother you," Shamika said as she took the seat opposite Michael.

"You're not bothering me. This is all for you anyway. I've been working nonstop for a few hours, I can take a break to talk to my favorite teenager."

Shamika giggled. "I think I'm the only teenager you know."

Michael laughed a hearty laugh, his first in weeks. "You got me there. I've never spent much time around children of any age but even if I had, you'd still be my favorite." Michael leaned back and laced his fingers behind his head. "So, tell me what's on your mind?"

"I want to meet her," Shamika said without preamble.

"You want to meet who?"

"You know who. My mom, I want to meet my real mom."

"Shamika are you sure? We have a lot going on with the trial right now. It's our turn starting tomorrow and I'll need you focused. I don't want you thinking about Syreeta when the jury will be studying everything about you."

Shamika nodded her head quickly. "Yes, I'm sure. I want to meet her as soon as possible. Tonight if we can."

Michael sat up straight and slowly ran his fingers through his hair. He opened his mouth then closed it. Seconds ticked away before he finally looked directly into Shamika's eyes as he spoke. "I take it you've given this a good deal of thought, and I don't want to upset you, but I have to ask. Why now? Why are you in such a hurry to meet your mother now when you've known about her for over a month?"

Shamika shifted her eyes to the floor, a habit Michael now knew as a dead giveaway for her insecurity. He wanted to press her for an answer but he knew from experience that would not be wise. Instead he sat patiently waiting for her to explain. It took nearly five minutes but she finally spoke.

"I'm scared. I know you and Kate and Aunt Nadine keep telling me everything is going to be fine, but you guys don't know that for sure. The jury might not believe me, and if that happens I'm going to prison for the rest of my life. Who will take care of my baby then? Aunt Nadine is old, and her cancer is back. She can't raise a baby."

"Cancer? What cancer?" Michael startled Shamika as he interrupted her.

Shamika clasped her hand over her mouth as her eyes grew wide.

"You've already started now, go ahead and finish," Michael said as he reached over and removed her hand from her mouth.

Shamika spoke again in a small voice. "She has cancer in her leg. She had it a couple years ago and it came back. She had some treatments though and they seem to be working."

Shamika added the last sentence with a youthful hopefulness that made Michael's heart soften. She really was just an innocent child. She had no business being on trial for murder or being concerned with her caregiver's cancer. "If you want to meet your mother tonight, I'll call her and arrange it but I need to speak with Nadine first. When you head back into the family room can you ask her to come in here please?"

Shamika stood without speaking and exited the room. Once she was gone Michael stood and began pacing the floor of the tiny room. He ran his fingers through his hair over and over again as he thought of the implications of Nadine having cancer. He knew something had been off about her but cancer never occurred to him. Cancer was for mean old bitter people, not loving and caring people like Nadine. He stopped pacing and closed his eyes for a moment as he tried to remember how to pray. If there was a

God, surely he wouldn't let Nadine die like his father had. He hated cancer. It had already taken so much from him.

"Why are you standing there with your eyes closed?" Nadine questioned as she entered the room limping slightly.

"I was praying…or at least trying to."

Nadine laughed as she took a seat at the table. "I never took you for the praying type," she said with a deep southern drawl.

"Well, normally I'm not but the thought of you having cancer will drive a man to desperate measures," Michael said with lowered eyes as he took a seat at the table as well.

"I knew that girl would slip up and tell you soon enough."

"Why didn't you tell me? Why would you put that secret on Shamika? Doesn't she have enough on her plate as it is?"

This time it was Nadine who lowered her eyes. "I never intended for her to find out either, but I had a couple bad days. The girl is smart. She figured it out and I just confirmed it."

"But why wouldn't you tell me so I could do something. I could have tried to find another placement for Shamika while you focused on your health."

"That's exactly why I didn't tell you. What Shamika needs more than anything else is stability. Uprooting her would have set us back months. Besides, the doctor caught it early this time. A couple rounds of chemo and radiation and I'm good as new."

"What about the cane and the limp?"

"The tumor is right above my knee. It's small but it's still a bugger. The thing makes pain shoot all the way up my leg when I put too much pressure on it. It's already going down though, so don't you worry about me," she said as she clasped her hands together. "This body has seen much worse, and if the tumor didn't stop me the first time it won't stop me this time."

Michael looked over at her as questions swirled around in his head. He wanted to bombard her with them all, but the look on her face told him she had just ended the conversation. He decided to go along with her for now and get to the more pressing matter at hand. "Shamika wants to meet Syreeta."

"See I told you she'd come around," Nadine said with a smile.

"She wants to meet her tonight."

Nadine's smile faded. "Why the rush?"

"She's afraid she might go to prison and she wants to make sure she has someone to take care of baby Adrian."

Nadine sighed heavily and allowed her shoulders to droop as the air left her body. This was a turn of events she was not prepared for. "For the record, I do not agree with this, but if it's what Shamika wants, I think you should set it up."

"I don't think the timing is great, but I agree we need to tread carefully with Shamika's feelings right now.

We need her as emotionally stable as possible before she takes the stand.

Three hours later, Nadine, Shamika, baby Adrian, Kate, Michael, and Syreeta all sat in a booth in a local 24 hour restaurant. No one was particularly hungry but they each ordered something anyway. As soon as the waitress was done taking orders, Syreeta, who'd been crying since they arrived, jumped right into conversation.

"I can't believe it's actually you," she said through her tears. "I've prayed so long that God would somehow bring you back to me but after all the years I started to think he wasn't listening to me."

Shamika gave a half smile. "It's good to meet you too. I'm sorry I refused to see you sooner. I was just so angry for what happened to me. I blamed you."

"Oh no baby. Don't apologize. It was my fault. If I had never run in that gas station none of this would have ever happened to you."

"That's just it. If none of it happened, I wouldn't have Adrian. And no matter what may come in the future, having Adrian is worth suffering on that mattress night after night."

The conversation went on for hours. Everyone at the table shed their fair share of tears, Michael included. The resilience and love Shamika encompassed was beyond what most people twice her age could even comprehend. The following day may be the start of a totally different life for her, but for the first time Michael felt Shamika was emotionally stable enough to handle it.

24

"All rise. Court is now in session. The Honorable Judge Nathan Harbison presiding."

"You may be seated."

There was a loud rumble in the courtroom as everyone took their seats. Michael turned to look behind him. The gallery was full. He shook his head at all of those so eager to watch a child be unlawfully persecuted. As he was turning his attention back towards the judge he caught a glimpse of someone, a very elegant someone that did not belong in a courtroom. His heart welled as his mother winked at him. He turned his attention back to the front feeling more prepared than he ever had in his life.

"Mr. Ayers you may call your first witness," Judge Harbison announced.

Michael spent his first day calling all of the boring character witnesses. Teachers, the school nurse, the pediatrician that hadn't seen Shamika since before puberty, and even Nadine. Witness after witness described Shamika as a withdrawn but well behaved teenager. No one had any remarkable memories of her, nor could they remember any friends she associated with. In short, Michael painted the picture of the little girl afraid to speak for fear she may suffer once she got home. In his mind the day went exactly as planned.

Later that evening as he prepared for another night on the lumpy couch of Jennings' baby's mama, Michael was startled by Higgins. "It's good to see you up and moving around, but can you say something instead of sneaking up on me" Michael said after he caught his breath.

"Sorry about that. Old habits die hard I guess. Look I need to run something by you."

"Sure," Michael said as they both took a seat on the sofa. "What's up?"

"You never asked me how I connected Kiplinger to Lamar."

"Yeah, how did you do that?"

Higgins handed Michael a piece of paper. Michael eyed what appeared to be a newspaper clipping carefully before unfolding it. Once he read it a smile spread across his face. This was it, the final nail in the coffin of the prosecution's case. He looked up at Higgins with glee.

"I don't know how you found this man, but you just saved that little girl's life. If there is anything I can ever do to repay you, please let me know."

Higgins smiled. "I was hoping you'd say that."

Defense Day 2

Shamika walked to the stand on shaky legs. She tried to remind herself of everything Michael and Kate had said but her mind became mush the second she heard her name called. She put her hand on the Bible and swore to tell the truth.

The truth is all I have, she thought.

Shamika took her seat inside the witness box and quickly scanned the crowd. In no time she found the people she was looking for, her mother and Nadine. Both women were smiling at her and willing her to relax with their eyes. They were her anchors, Kate had explained more times than she could count. If things got hairy during cross examination she was to find her anchors and focus in on them.

Michael's questions were straightforward. He asked Shamika about her childhood and life living with Lamar and Lydia. He asked her if she ever felt they weren't her natural parents. He asked her about the night Lamar was stabbed and what went through her mind during the assault. She shed tears while she answered but for the most part her answers were clear and concise, the result of weeks of preparation. Once Michael completed his direct examination all of the warm and fuzzies went out the window. Bart came for blood.

"Shamika you testified that you did not know Lamar and Lydia were not your natural parents, correct?"

"Yes," Shamika replied with a shaky voice.

"Then tell me, how is it your guidance counselor from sixth grade, A Mrs…..Hood," Bart said after referring to his notes, "How is it Mrs. Hood remembers you saying Lamar didn't act like a real daddy?"

Shamika's eyes shot to Michael's and then to Kate's. Her pulse quickened slightly. "I…..I don't remember saying that, but…"

"Objection Your Honor, hearsay," Michael yelled before Shamika could finish her sentence.

"I'll withdraw the question." Bart quickly responded.

He walked over to his table and retrieved a stack of photos. He approached Shamika with the gruesome crime scene photos. "Shamika, you said you don't remember much about the moments after you stabbed Lamar. Looking at these pictures, do they ring a bell?"

Shamika's hand shot up to her mouth and tears flooded her face. "I wasn't trying to kill him. I just didn't want him to kill my baby."

"So the pictures do jog your memory?"

Shamika looked around the courtroom trying desperately to find her anchors. Everything was blurry because of her tears. She tried to take a deep breath like Kate taught her but her throat felt like it was closing.

"Do you remember calling 911 Shamika?"

Shamika's eyes shot to Bart's. She didn't remember calling 911. She thought Lydia called before she left.

"Your Honor, I'd like to play for the court Exhibit M, a recording retained by the State this morning in which Shamika Carrington is heard calling to report the stabbing."

"Objection," Michael yelled angrily as he stood. "Your Honor this is the first we are hearing about this so-called recording. We have not been given the opportunity to examine its authenticity."

"Your Honor I can assure you the tape is in fact authentic. Mr. Ayers has had the same access to public records as my office has. In fact this tape was discovered only moments ago by an intern in the D.A's office. Had the defense done their due diligence they would have found it too."

"Overruled," Judge Harbison roared. Mr. Winslow continue with your questioning.

An angry Michael plopped into his chair and began making notes. This was yet another grounds for appeal should it come down to that. Although with his discovery last night, he doubted very seriously Shamika would be convicted. However, he still hadn't heard the tape.

"911 what's your emergency?"

The entire courtroom was on edge as Bart played the recorded phone call.

"I stabbed him."

"Ma'am who did you stab?"

"That bastard. I stabbed him and now he's dead."

"Ma'am, tell me your name."

Dial tone.

The courtroom erupted as soon as the tape ended. Judge Harbison had to bang his gavel five times and threaten to clear the gallery before everyone settled down. Bart seized the shock of the moment.

"Shamika, you sounded very angry on that call. Are you sure stabbed Lamar in self-defense or were you getting back at him for something else?"

Shamika was sobbing uncontrollably but she managed to get out a few audible words. "I was only protecting my baby. He had the hanger. He was going to kill him."

"Objection! Your Honor, my client clearly needs a moment to gather herself. She's a child for Christ's sake."

Judge Harbison banged his gavel at Michael. "Objection overruled. Ms. Carrington you are instructed to answer Mr. Winslow's question."

Bart took the opportunity to repeat himself. "Shamika, did you stab Lamar because you were angry at him for kidnapping you when you were a baby?"

It took a moment for her to respond, but when she did her answer was more convincing than anything she's said all day. "For all I knew Lamar was my daddy. And my daddy raped me. He raped me all the time and when I couldn't fake blood for my period anymore he figured out I was pregnant. He tried to stick a clothes hanger in me and I grabbed the knife and stabbed him. He was a mean bastard but that's not why I stabbed him. It was either him or my baby. I chose my baby."

"One last question Shamika, why did you have a knife by your bed?"

"Because I knew he was coming."

Michael hung his head at her answer. Kate closed her eyes and tried to hide her emotions. Bart was as smug as ever.

"No further questions Your Honor."

"You may step down Ms. Carrington. Court is in recess until 1pm," Judge Harbison banged his gavel ending the grueling morning session.

Lunch flew by and the afternoon spectators greatly outnumbered the morning ones. News of Shamika's testimony spread so quickly the bailiffs had to police the doors to the courtroom to ensure the room was not over capacity. Despite the travesty of Shamika's cross examination, Michael felt confident that after he called his final witness there was no way the jury would convict Shamika. He hadn't bothered to subpoena the witness or notify Bart. He knew the witness would be in the courtroom just as he always had been, and he couldn't wait to see the surprise on Bart's face when he announced the witness.

"All rise, court is now in session. The Honorable Judge Nathan Harbison is presiding."

"You may be seated. Ok, Mr. Ayers, call your next witness."

Michael stood. "Your Honor, the defense calls Mr. John Kiplinger."

The sounds of the reaction of the gallery was deafening. Michael struggled to hide his contentment as Bart shot to his feet to object.

"Your Honor, we have been given no notice of this witness."

"We only just learned of his involvement during lunch Your Honor," Michael said stealing Bart's own tactic.

Judge Harbison banged his gavel. "I see where this is going so let me be very clear on this. Mr. Kiplinger will be the last surprise witness allowed to testify during this trial. Do we understand each other gentlemen?"

Michael and Bart both mumbled their agreeance, but only one of them was pleased. John Kiplinger strode purposefully to the witness stand buttoning his jacket as he walked. The room all marveled at what the chief of police could possibly add to the case. Once he was sworn in Kiplinger shot daggers at Michael with his eyes. Michael ignored him.

"Mr. Kiplinger, I understand you are a very busy man so I'll get right to the point. How did you know the deceased Mr. Lamar Carrington?"

"Carrington and I served in the Army together. We were good buddies many moons ago."

"So the two of you have not kept up with each other over the years?"

"We've met for dinner a few times over the years but we haven't remained in constant contact."

"So from what you know of Lamar, can you give the court any information regarding his character?"

"When I knew Lamar he was an outstanding soldier and he took care of his buddies."

"And what do you mean by take care?"

"I mean if he saw a man in need and he could help, Lamar would step in and help."

"Did that include women?"

"I beg your pardon?"

"Women. Did Lamar Carrington help his buddies, as you call them, secure women?"

"I don't know what you're talking about."

"I think you do. Your Honor I'd like to present Exhibit N into evidence."

"Let me review it first," Judge Harbison replied. The judge took the document and took his time reading over it. He handed it back to Michael with a skeptical glance. "Let the record show exhibit N is being entered into evidence. You may proceed Mr. Ayers."

"Judge, can the exhibit be placed on the screen for viewing?"

"Yes, Bailiff can you please…"

Before the judge could finish his request the bailiff was moving and had the document set up on the screen in no time. Michael was delighted on the inside. If for no other reason, he knew what this was doing to Bart.

"Mr. Kiplinger, can you read the headline of the article displayed on the screen?"

John Kiplinger was so angry Michael thought his eyes were going to bulge out of his head. His mouth twitched as he read the headline aloud. "Soldiers accused of rape face charges in German court."

"Mr. Kiplinger can you tell me who the headline is referring to?"

"We were acquitted."

"That's not what I asked you. I asked for you to tell me who the headline if referring to."

"Lamar and me."

"So while you and Mr. Carrington were serving in the Army together in Germany, you were arrested and charged with raping a young female soldier. Is that correct?"

"Yes, but I never raped anyone which is why we were acquitted and our records expunged."

"I understand the outcome of the case, but I do have a few questions concerning the event that led up to the charges."

"Objection!" Bart shouted as loud as he could. "A twenty year old case has nothing to do with why we're here today."

"I'll allow the question. Overruled," Judge Harbison bellowed as though he were annoyed by Bart's interruption.

Michael continued. "How did you come into contact with the young woman that accused the two of you of rape?"

"She was dating Lamar."

"She was his girlfriend?"

"I don't know. All I know is that night she was on a date with him."

"Okay, so how did the act of intercourse happen?"

"We all drank too much at the club off post. We had to take a cab back to the barracks. In the cab Lamar and the girl were making out pretty hot and heavy. When we got back to the barracks I sat outside the room on the floor while the two of them went inside. After a while I knocked on the door. I needed a pillow. Lamar came to the door with a goofy smile on his face and asked me if I wanted a turn. I was drunk and when I peeked around his shoulder the girl was staring at me like she wanted me to come in there. I went in, we had sex and then the next thing I knew she said we raped her."

"So you maintain that the girl never said no or asked you to stop."

"She never said no or did anything that led me to believe she didn't want it. If she had I would have stopped."

"You would huh?" Michael chuckled as he went in for the kill. "When was the last time you saw Lamar Carrington?"

"I'm not sure, two maybe three years ago."

Michael crossed his arms as he studied Kiplinger. "I'm sure I don't have to tell you the implications of lying under oath. I'm going to ask you again to give you the opportunity to correct that last answer. When was the last time you saw Lamar Carrington?"

"As I already stated, it was roughly two or three years ago."

Michael walked back to his table and picked up a file. "Your Honor I was hoping the chief of police would be honest but since he is not, I have additional evidence that I would like to present to the court."

"Objection! This is getting outrageous. The defense should have presented all evidence associated with this witness when the witness was introduced."

"Your Honor I had no way of knowing the chief of police would lie under oath."

Judge Harbison banged his gavel. "That's enough! Both of you approach the bench." When Michael and Bart were close enough to hear him whisper Judge Harbison continued. "Mr. Ayers are you sure you want to accuse the chief of police of perjury? This could have serious implications for our local judicial system."

"Your Honor, I just want the truth to come out. And I have proof right here from the security camera of a neighbor that John Kiplinger was at the Carrington home a few months before the murder, the night of the murder while the police were collecting evidence, and again about a month ago."

"Mr. Kiplinger is not on trial here," Bart interjected. "His presence at the Carrington home doesn't change whether or not Shamika Carrington premeditated the murder of her father."

Judge Harbison held up his hand. He looked at Michael. "Let me take a look at the pictures." The judge took a long hard look at each photo. "And the owner of the home is available to testify to the validity of the pictures?"

"Yes Your Honor. He's here in the courtroom."

"Okay. I will allow the pictures into evidence. You may both step back."

Michael returned to questioning Kiplinger once the photos were displayed for the jurors to view.

"Mr. Kiplinger, here is a photo of you entering the Carrington home approximately 11 months ago. Does that jog your memory?"

Kiplinger shocked the courtroom with his reply. "Your Honor I plead the fifth."

25

Michael, Kate, and Shamika sat at the defense table waiting impatiently for the jury to be led into the courtroom. Judge Harbison had already given his expectations for how everyone was to behave once the verdict was read, but everyone knew emotion would overrule those expectations. Michael looked over at Shamika with a furrowed brow. She was so young and still so fragile. Life in prison without the possibility of parole was too much for anyone, but for a sixteen year old…it would be devastating. Shamika turned as if she felt the heat of his stare.

"I'm going to be okay," she whispered. "Even if they don't believe me. I know Adrian will be okay with my mother and if I was put in the same situation I would do it all over again to protect my baby."

Michael felt a lump form in the back of his throat. He blinked rapidly trying to hold the tears in. Kate spoke up trying to draw his attention.

"Michael, hold it together. Remember why we're here. You laid out one hell of a case. You have to trust that the jury saw through the lies and saw the truth about Lamar and Kiplinger."

"My faith in humanity is a little low right now."

Shamika reached for his hand and squeezed it. "If I can still believe, so can you."

Michael nodded at his client and closed his eyes for a moment. His stomach was doing somersaults and he needed a moment to settle himself before the jury entered the room. His moment was cut short by the sound of screaming from the back of the room.

"Gun!" Someone yelled in a high pitched tone.

Then the shots started ringing. Three maybe four gun shots in quick succession. Michael's thoughts registered more slowly than he expected. The room around him started to quickly fade at the corners. He wanted to reach out for Shamika, to dive to protect Kate, to shield the women from the gun fire, but the black was closing in on him. He vaguely heard the sound of Kate's voice. He felt something, a hand on his chest maybe. Kate's hand? He couldn't be sure, couldn't hear her well enough to make out what she was saying. He fought to keep his eyes open, willing himself to avoid the overwhelming desire to welcome the darkness. Shamika. Where was Shamika? He couldn't hear or see her. Did she get hit like he did? He called out her name, but no sound came out. He tried again but nothing. He tried a third time, with a faint whistling sound escaping his lips.

"She's safe Michael. Don't try to talk. Hang in there," Kate said to him.

At the sound of her soothing tone Michael closed his eyes and succumbed to the darkness.

Epilogue

Nadine, Syreeta, and Kate all sat waiting impatiently to hear the news that was so important they had to stop what they were doing and rush over only to find the office empty. The six months following the shooting were the worst any of them had ever experienced. It's not every day a police chief opens fire on a crowded courtroom. John Kiplinger killed four people and wounded two others before turning the gun on himself. It was the bloodiest scene ever to hit a Charlotte, North Carolina courtroom; and thanks to the media that was there covering the trial, the murders made national headlines. Experts speculated John cracked under the pressure of his secrets being revealed, others blamed Michael for twisting the situation to get a criminal acquitted. No matter which side folks chose to believe one fact remained, the name Michael Ayers would forever be remembered and the Carrington case would be studied for years to come.

"Hi everyone," Shamika said as she bounced into the room. Since being acquitted of all charges her entire demeanor changed. She was the typical teenager in many ways, but because of all she'd experienced, she was also very mature and responsible. She'd finished high school through correspondence courses and was going to start community college in the fall. Her life wasn't a bed of roses, but since moving in with her mother she was experiencing love for the first time. It showed in her smile.

Michael walked in behind Shamika wearing a smile of his own. The last six months for him were no cake walk. John Kiplinger shot Michael three times, two shots hitting his left arm and the third grazing the top of his left shoulder. The first or second bullet, doctors couldn't be sure which, had torn through his bicep ripping the muscle to shreds. He'd undergone emergency surgery and months of rigorous physical therapy but his prognosis was promising. In another couple of months provided he continued his therapy workouts, he'd be as good as new.

"Hey there. I'm sorry if I scared you ladies asking you to rush over here like this but Shamika and I have some exciting news we'd like to share," Michael said still splashing that 100 watt smile.

"So, as you know Michael has been working on getting me and baby Adrian taken care of financially since Kiplinger is dead now. Well, the settlement from his estate came in today! Adrian will have a trust fund to pay for his college and I'll get monthly payments to help me take care of him!"

Shamika gushed as all of the ladies in the room exclaimed their excitement for her. Being a single mother was expensive, being the single mother of a child whose father went postal and shot up a court room before killing himself was astronomical.

"Wait, there's more," she said still smiling. "Mom, Michael worked out a settlement for you too. The State of South Carolina is going to pay you $2 million dollars for your wrongful conviction."

Syreeta's mouth dropped to the floor. "$2 million, Michael that's too much. I wouldn't know what to do with all of that money."

"It's okay," he assured her. "I'll help you get it all set up so that you can live off of it for the rest of your life. If you ask me, $2 million is only a drop in the bucket but that's the most I could get without going to trial. And I know all of you can understand why this group is not ready for another trial."

Syreeta clasped her hands together. Tears rolled down her face as she spoke. "I can't tell you how many times I sat in that cell and prayed for God to make things right. I knew he'd answer me eventually but I wasn't expecting this."

Michael stared at her while she drank it all in. No more cleaning filthy hotel rooms which despite Higgins' claims otherwise, Michael knew were heavily used for prostitution. He could only imagine the types of things she's seen while she cleaned. His eyes wandered to Nadine who'd now placed her arms around Syreeta. Nadine still played a big part in both Shamika and

Syreeta's lives. She'd retired from her job as a social worker to focus exclusively on them. She knew the two of them would need the support after being apart for so long, but most importantly she felt her job was done. She'd seen enough Shamikas to last a lifetime, but none of them meant more to her than the one she had the pleasure of loving now.

Michael's eyes traveled to the last person in the room. His Kate. Yes, she was his. During his recovery from the shooting Kate and his mother had fussed over him nonstop. He wasn't comfortable having his mother around so much, but Kate...Kate was like air. Having her there with him day in and day out confirmed what he already knew. He cleared his throat before he spoke again.

"I have one last announcement. I have finally cleared up all of the necessary legalities concerning the firm and the name has officially been changed to Ayers & Ayers."

Kate tilted her head and questioned him with her eyes.

"You," he said with a smile as he closed the distance between them. "The other Ayers is you, if you'll have me." And there right in front of their nuclear family Michael dropped to one knee presenting Kate with a flawless emerald cut diamond. "Will you marry me Kate?"

"Of course I will," she exclaimed as she threw her arms around him forgetting all about his injuries. Pain shot through him but Michael didn't flinch. He simply stood and planted a kiss on the lips of the woman he loved.

Note to Reader:

I hope you have enjoyed reading this book. In my opinion it is my most poignant piece to date. It took me two years of writing, scrapping, and re-writing to tell the story in a way that would not only entertain but bring light to social issues here in America and abroad.

While Shamika Carrington is a fictional character and most cases do not include all of the things we experienced through this character, these are very real issues children and teenagers face. Child abduction, abuse, neglect, sexual exploitation, teenage pregnancy, and harsh punishments for crimes committed by teenagers who felt their backs were against the wall are all issues that need to be addressed. Every voice that speaks on behalf of a child is valuable. We may not have all of the answers, but together we can make our world a better place for future generations.

Sincerely,

O.R. Johnson

Printed in Great Britain
by Amazon

37886586R00244